DRAGON
DAUGHTER

DRAGON
DAUGHTER

STEVEN ARMSTRONG

atmosphere press

For Asa Ace.
You're next. I can't wait to see what stories you unleash.
Love you.

I.

The night was quiet, the air was cool, and the water was calm at the river that ran along the edge of the town of Mysteya. A hooded old woman wrapped in long gray robes with golden loops embroidered on them walked along a smooth dirt pathway near the river's edge. She stopped for a moment to let the gentle breeze hit her face as she looked up at the stars, drawing her hood behind her ear.

Nighttime walks were typical for Séya when she couldn't sleep. She found the stars in the clear night sky comforting. Seeing them quietly twinkling made her less lonesome. She liked to believe that each star contained the spirits of her loved ones, and over the course of more than a century of her life, many left lasting impressions upon her heart. Too few of those special people were left now for her to connect with. She considered this and continued her walk along the moonlit pathway.

Suddenly, there was a thud against the rocky shore. Muffled sounds that Séya couldn't decipher were coming from the same direction. However, she thought nothing of the noises at first, merely wrapping herself more tightly in her garments as she moved along. The commotion became louder as she edged closer, yet the sounds couldn't break through whatever was keeping them in. She stopped, scanned the river, and realized the ruckus was coming from below.

As she peered over the edge of the rocks, Séya decided to see what all the fuss was about. Carefully, the old woman walked off of the dirt pathway and climbed down the large pieces of fragmented earth formations until she reached the lowest one. Séya noticed a closed basket made of wicker floating on the surface of the water. It was stuck between two rocks, pushed and pulled back and forth by the current. The racket Séya heard came from inside the vessel and seemed more dramatic, like a screeching pronouncement of danger.

She lifted her long robes, knelt, and pulled the tightly closed top off the basket. Her eyes widened at what she discovered; a brief tingling of butterflies danced in her stomach.

Séya wasn't particularly nervous, more stunned than anything else to find her eyes resting upon a small baby inside the canvas-lined container, wrapped in a thick, beige blanket.

Hands and feet flailing around under the woolen covering in a fit, the little person seemed a self-contained universe of life in all its vastness and infinite possibilities. Far beyond the known world, beyond even the sun, the moon, and stars that Séya found so reassuring.

She looked on, mesmerized by the little one, who was both familiar and foreign at the same time. Séya gently caressed the small head, feeling the dark silken poof of curly hair. She noticed that nary a drop of water could be found on the child, save the tears that streamed back to the baby's ears, which glistened in the dim moonlight.

Séya pulled the basket from the river and carried it back up to the pathway where she tried to calm the child. She took the baby out and cradled it. Back and forth, the old woman rocked slightly, as if engaged in a slow dance. The baby didn't seem to weigh very much; no larger than a small bag of grains, like the kind Séya might pick up from the market. If she had to guess, the child was half a year old. The more she thought on that, the more she wondered how something so darling, something so beyond price, could have been left unattended.

"Shhh, little one," she said to the child, gently caressing the baby's smooth and chilled face, a golden brown like leaves at the start of autumn.

It seemed to work for a moment, and the child grew quieter. She looked into the baby's eyes, a warm brown like hers. They seemed to be scanning the old woman's face for something.

Séya could see the brighter stars reflected in the eyes of the small face and released a deep sigh, looking to the sky as if she thought the baby might have been sent from above. "Did you come from up there?" Séya spoke softly. "Are you a child of the stars or a piece of the sky?"

The child continued to make incoherent sounds in between half-cries.

Séya smiled warmly. "A piece of the lovely sky it is then," she said. "And an adorable skylet you are."

Of course, the baby hadn't really come from the sky. Séya liked the idea that some spirit from above had come down to keep her company even if for a short while. It was a heartening notion. She gently placed the baby back into the open basket and made sure the child was snugly packed before she closed it again and carried it away.

2.

Séya arrived at her small home, which consisted only of two rooms. One she slept in, the other was her living space. Attached was a small kitchen.

She placed the wicker basket in the center of a compact round oak table and sat down in a faded red cushioned armchair near it. Before getting too comfortable, Séya removed the lid from the basket and saw that the child was now asleep. She sat and pondered over what she might do with the baby for the evening. She couldn't very well keep it, and she began to worry because she had no food for the little one should he or she wake up in the middle of the night.

And just what was the story of this child? Was it a boy or a girl? Séya hadn't the heart to look while the child slept. Where were the parents, and how was it that the baby came to be in the river?

As she mulled over these questions, there was only one place the old woman thought to take the baby, but it was late in the evening and she didn't want to be a bother. Séya figured a cup of tea might calm her mind and help her decide what to do next.

She moved to the kitchen area, where she put a black

kettle full of water on top of a small makeshift stove constructed from four concrete blocks designed to make a square. In the center of the cubic construct were many bits of broken tree branches and twigs. Séya took two small wooden sticks from a glass jar that sat on a shelf just above the stove and stuck them among the short tree limbs, rubbing them together to make a fire.

She stood quietly listening to the crackling flames and the relaxed breathing of a little person only feet away from her. The more she pondered, the more her mind wandered to a place she mostly visited under cover of darkness. For many years, it was only rumored to exist. Somewhere at the edges of Mysteya lay something mysterious; few cared enough to uncover the secrets behind it. Séya was the only living person who knew the truth and knew how to get there. That night, she seriously considered making an emergency visit.

She continued to think and allowed her mind to take her back to her youth. She was a different person back then, known as a free spirit, endlessly open to new places, people, and experiences. Séya was tremendously popular among her peers and elders alike. If ever a person was in trouble or needed a friend, Séya wouldn't be far away. Her caring heart was expansive.

One of Mysteya's great young midwives and healers, she impressed her instructors and came to teach many groups of students in the healing arts and midwifery. She was one of the few in the town who could welcome new life while providing comfort for those transitioning into the afterlife.

Séya seemed to possess endless warmth. The aura surrounding her was palpable enough to affect everything from the vegetation that seemed to perk up when she was near, to the very air that began to feel fresher as she passed through it. The people near her also became more jovial and genuinely pleasant.

Boys especially took a liking to her, and she genuinely liked and remained kind to them. Aside from the few she called her friends, Séya mostly kept to herself. The boys always offered to carry heavy items for her from the market and told her how beautiful she was. They spoke of the wild curls in her mysteriously cool gray hair that protruded from underneath the earth-toned head cap she wore. The exposed spirals made them curious about whether it was possible to tame them. They told her how her eyes were like mahogany and how her face and skin glowed like fireflies in the night, speaking the language of light and sending signals out for companionship.

But Séya had a secret.

One she could never expect those boys to comprehend. She possessed unexplainable magical power. With her maturation came the instinctive understanding, like prey knows a predator, that otherworldly beings, human or creature, were in near-constant danger. Fear of persecution kept them on the fringes, cast out of their communities. A sense developed within Séya that she was connected to a plane of existence that linked her to others who understood magic. The thought was comforting, yet saddening. She knew magical beings kept their true selves a secret, something she found isolating.

One particular being she often sensed when going about her day, came to her at times in dreams when she slept. Séya could never see it, but she came to feel whenever her chest grew warm and goosebumps rippled across her shoulders, that the spirit was calling to her. It wasn't an anxious call; at least it didn't feel that way. It was more like the warm greeting of an old friend, tender and familiar.

As she slept one night, Séya dreamt of herself sitting in the middle of a vast meadow, marveling at the sight of a sea of sparkling stars. She was relaxed until suddenly a giant shaggy-haired boar triple the size of a person, appeared behind her.

She turned and looked up to see the massive beast looking back at her.

Breath shot from its large nostrils, disrupting the blades of grass below, and immediately, Séya jumped up from her spot and ran as fast as she could.

The boar gave chase and gained speed. It got so close she could feel its hot breath against the top of her head.

Just when she thought the beast would crush her, she looked up into the sky and suddenly felt a warm sensation in her chest. Simultaneously, a large orb of light appeared above her; it flickered to its own deliberate rhythm, like an unflustered heartbeat. She didn't see where it came from, but Séya recognized that the orb of light came from the sky. It didn't scare away the boar as she hoped it might. Instead, something else happened as she continued to run.

She was pulled upward from the surface of the meadow by some force.

The boar jumped; Séya felt its shaggy hair brush against her feet, but she was out of its reach. Closer and closer she got to the light until she woke up, untroubled.

She heard the call of the magical spirit once again and wondered how she might respond or make contact somehow.

For a time, no one suspected anything. Life went on as usual in Mysteya. The town thrived, and aside from occasional skirmishes with neighboring communities, all was well.

Until suddenly, a deadly plague swept through, swiftly claiming many lives. New babies and the elderly were especially vulnerable, and it weighed heavily on Séya that she could not save everyone. Losing the babies particularly hurt her. She thought of the adventures they would never have and the futures they would never see. The passing of the elderly felt like the loss of collective histories to her. The two generations would never connect. One denied young spirits to pass on their knowledge and wisdom to, while the other would never encounter those who would guide them along some of life's most uncertain paths.

Survivors of the dark time began to grow suspicious of the healers as few of them suffered symptoms, and even fewer of them died. Why had they emerged from the crisis unscathed?

It wasn't long before Mysteya's town council led an investigation into the activities of the healers. Being a key instructor, Séya was directly accused of witchcraft, prompting all the children who survived the plague, especially those that she had helped birth, to be thoroughly examined for contamination.

She returned to herself in the kitchen and shook her head as the water began to boil in the small cauldron. The thought of being accused of contaminating babies still stung her heart.

Séya looked into the main room where the baby slept and let out a sigh, wondering what the council members and the townspeople of old Mysteya would say if they knew a little person was in her home. Séya had far outlived many who would have heard of her being accused of witchcraft. As a sorceress, she aged very slowly. She took some comfort in the fact that they weren't around to continue spreading fear about her power.

After years of self-imposed exile, she returned to a very different town than the one she left, and it took some time for her to feel comfortable in the new identity she crafted for herself. Old Mysteya knew her as a respected healer. She was now the strange wandering lady.

But as she grabbed a cup and prepared the tea leaves, she resigned herself to the thought that those from old Mysteya wouldn't say much at all were they alive. Not with words anyway. They would probably move swiftly to kill her as they had tried once before.

After one sleepless night and a very long morning of treating many sick people, Séya sought rest at Crescent Lake, a secluded area she was fond of visiting when she could. Every so often, she would see the occasional deer or squirrel moving around the large crescent-shaped body of water. Other than that, she was mostly alone with her thoughts.

She stripped down to her undergarments and climbed into the warm water. Close to the lake's edge, Séya attempted to relax as best she could. Several times, she submerged herself beneath the surface as if to cleanse her whole being of the sweat, dirt, sickness, and deaths of those who didn't survive the night.

As she prepared to leave the lake, Séya was lost in thought about other people who would come to need care when she returned to her post. While dressing herself, they came for her from the depths of the forest.

Like a quiet mist, a small group of townspeople converged upon the area.

"Witch," spat a burly man who led the group.

Startled, Séya turned to face him.

Silence.

The two stared at each other before she blinked, and in that instant, Séya calmed her nerves as best she could. "I'm sorry," she said. Her hands grabbed the cool gray waves of hair draped over one shoulder, and squeezed out water. "I'm afraid I don't understand."

Séya stepped back and bent down to collect her earth-toned head cap when she noticed a shovel in the hands of another man among the group.

The burly man seemed to foam at the mouth; his exposed teeth and dark, unkempt beard made him resemble a wild animal ready to strike. He deliberately pulled a large hunting blade from a sheath strapped to his side. "You understand this," he said gruffly.

The others slowly stepped in closer.

Séya put on her head cap and turned around to see how she might escape. "Please," she began, "I must return to the infirmary."

"You will not contaminate our children," said another hardwearing woman with an old, rough-looking rope in her calloused hands, who Séya recognized as the grandmother of children she once cared for. One of the few female members of the local hunting group in town, she would not be easy to escape from.

"Roesia," Séya protested equably. "Please, let us speak civilly."

There was no response.

Séya let out a deep breath and felt a sudden, subtle

warmth in her stomach that moved upward. She placed her hand to her bosom just as the warmth reached that area. It was as if her heart was heating up and would burst into flames at a moment's notice.

She wasted no more time; stone-faced, Séya broke into a run.

She wasn't fearful at that moment; she had a one-track mind to break through the group and get back to town. Shaking the grasp of one of the men, she whizzed past another before tripping over herself, hands and knees greeting the earth.

It was the moment the group needed to gain on her.

Séya picked herself up and got only two steps before she was struck in the head by a long, thick stick made of hickory wood. The earth-toned cap flew off, exposing her wild curls, still wet from the lake, as her body hit the grass with a muffled thud.

"Where's your magic now," said one member of the group declaratively, as they surveyed her motionless body.

Blood began to flow from the back of her head as they knelt to handle her.

"Turn her over and hold her hands! Quickly!"

"Tie her up!"

In the last vestige of consciousness, Séya saw nothing. Her body felt hot, as though she spent the day basking in the sun's warm rays.

As the group poked and prodded her, preparing to collect and take her away, Séya heard a voice in the darkness.

I am here.

She couldn't be sure whether or not the voice was something she created at that moment to give her hope that she could save herself, yet the voice was clear, true.

"Help Bondon lift her!" exclaimed Roesia to a tall, blonde-haired participant who was slender in stature.

"He can carry her over his shoulder," said the young man defiantly. "He needs no help from—" He suddenly fell silent.

The burly leader of the group noticed. "What, boy," he said.

Séya could barely make out the conversation. Before she gave in to the comfort of oblivion, she heard the blonde young man begin to scream a warning.

The words never came out.

Something large hit the ground with the force of a downed, old and large tree, rich with the history of time; the earth rumbled as if overrun by large boars like the one Séya dreamt of. This time, she was in no condition to run away. She would have to suffer whatever consequence that lay ahead for her.

Grunts and shouts came from the group as they scurried about in a flurry. The tools and weapons they had for Séya now clanked and struck against tough surfaces as bodies fell to the ground. The commotion culminated in a thunderous rumbling and a bloodcurdling howl from one person in the group.

Séya thought she heard a hint of something sizzling, then passed into nothingness.

I am here.

That day, Séya was indebted to an unlikely ally, a kindred spirit of magic she had sensed before the two ever met. Their dynamic would become more than she could have imagined. Considering that, and the innocent life now in her care, Séya finally decided on a course of action.

She would have a cup of tea, and then she would take

the child to *her*.

3.

Séya placed her empty teacup on the round oak table and grabbed a scarf, wrapping herself quickly when she saw the baby begin to stir in the basket, quietly making noises in its sleep. She wondered for a moment if the child might be in some deep dream, then she grabbed a blanket from a small tan-colored couch in the middle of the room and covered the infant. Séya knew that the trip would be particularly challenging, carrying a large basket, and it was sure to be colder once she left her home. She threw her hood over her head, grabbed the basket, and set off on her journey.

A chilly wind picked up. Séya put the top back onto the wicker basket tightly and grabbed the handle. She walked down the slight hill and onto the main road.

As she neared the end of the path, she noticed the dark outline of a stout man, not quite middle-aged yet sitting outside his home in a wooden chair having a drink. He looked warm and comfortable in his dark hat and a dark jacket.

When he saw Séya approaching, he removed his hat. She glanced over and could barely make out his face by the light of two oil lamps that hung on either side of the doorway to his home. His beard was just at the point beyond stubble, and the top of his nose had a dent in it from a childhood injury.

He raised his bottle in acknowledgement of her. "If it isn't Silly Old Séya," he said gruffly, taking a sip of his drink. "How are you on this fine evening?"

"Good evening to you, Willard," she replied as calmly as she could, gripping the handle of the basket more tightly and walking at a slower pace. "Isn't it a little late for you to be up?"

"I might ask you the same," he said. "You ought to be careful out here."

"I'll be fine; I know this place very well," she replied. "After all, it has been my home since before you were born."

Séya once knew Willard's family well, as she did most of the families of old Mysteya whose children came to her care at birth. He was the youngest child of a woman who was one of the last babies Séya came into contact with before her exile. Willard's mother passed away, never making any mention of Séya to her children.

She didn't want any association with a witch.

Willard chuckled and stood up from the wooden chair he sat in. "What have you there in the basket?" he asked.

"Flowers," she said. Just then, the baby coughed.

"Sounds like more than just flowers," Willard said, taking another drink.

"And a baby raccoon," she said quickly. "Knocked out cold. Found him rummaging through my garden. Somehow, they get in every now and again, you understand."

"Rummaging through your garden, or rummaging

through your secret special healing plants that ward off those imaginary creatures you always tell the kiddies about?" Willard asked, amused.

"That's right," Séya replied, almost dismissively. Sometimes she had to concentrate hard on selling her strangeness. "I'll be on my way now, Willard."

"Headed into the woods for another blood sacrifice to the spirits?" He was beginning to have fun with the old woman. "Poor baby raccoon. At least you've brought flowers for its grave."

"Oh, I'm hoping for two sacrifices tonight," she said. "Once this baby goes, the mother will be next. You can be sure she's tracking us right now." Séya looked over her shoulder quickly as if in a paranoid state.

"Right then, better hurry before it gets even later," said Willard as he took another drink.

"Good night, Willard," she said. "Look out for that mother raccoon! Don't want her ruining your yard!" Séya moved swiftly beyond the road and through the brush leading into the forest.

Like most in the town, Willard believed Séya to be a crazy old lady who was losing her mind, and that's just how she liked it. It wouldn't do for the townspeople to know too much about her. Certain private details getting out would mean trouble for her way of life, and she couldn't have that. That this baby had come to her was as much a worrisome surprise as it was a pleasant one. It had been ages since she was in contact with a child and her heart felt warm at the thought of carrying something so precious again.

In a different life, she may have wanted to keep the child and have someone to take care of, someone to teach and protect. But then, living with a baby would bring her much unwanted attention. People would start asking questions out of concern for the child's wellbeing around the local town loony, "Silly Old Séya." The infant would most certainly be taken away.

Even worse, if word got out that she was also a sorceress, the consequences would be dire for them both. Séya would be hanged, and the baby burned just for being associated with her.

She moved through the forest with the skill of a stealthy wolf as she hopped over logs and small streams, side-stepping boulders, and bushes. After clearing the woods, she came to the foothill of a mountain. It was nothing she wasn't used to, but she found herself adjusting her movements to accommodate the basket from which muffled sounds were now coming. The baby was once again wide awake.

Up she hiked until she reached a pathway that stuck out of the side of the mountain, which curved to her left. She followed it around the side until she reached a rock platform that stood out with bushes on the surface. Just behind it was a large crack in the mountain. She placed the basket on the platform and pushed it as close to the bushes as she could before trying to climb up herself.

The child was crying now, irritated by all the moving around.

"Shhh, child," she said as soothingly as she could through grunting sounds as she made her way to the basket.

The old woman moved through the bushes and into the crack of the mountain. Séya had to crouch her head slightly to make it inside, but once she was in, she moved carefully as there was little light to guide her through the tunnel. The farther she went, the darker the cave became. She wasn't too concerned, though, having made the trip enough times that she had by now committed the path to memory. The baby's loud cries reverberated through the walls of the cave as she went deeper.

Séya continued down rocky hills and through complex tunnel structures until finally, she reached her destination: a wide-open chamber. The soothing sounds of waterfalls nearby and the child's incoherent babbling was a strange musical marriage to Séya; she noticed the little one was beginning to calm down somewhat as if to purposely listen to the new refrain the falls created.

The floor was mostly smooth earth and granite, with the exception of several cracks. Séya stepped onto an uneven circular bed of grass in the center of the cave floor, where she placed the basket and removed the top. The baby stopped making noises momentarily, taking in the sight of all the shadows and dark spaces.

The old woman raised her right hand, and several wall-mounted torches surrounding the area where she stood slowly came to life. The feeble flames danced tentatively at first. When a moment passed, they became brighter and more alive. There was now sufficient light.

"Are you awake?" she called out, her voice echoing.

There was no answer.

"I need to speak with you about something."

Silence.

Soon, there was a heavy shuffling sound; something was stirring.

A grumbly, groggy voice answered her. "It's late, dear Séya. What is it?"

"Please come see," she said.

The shuffling slowly became louder and gave way to heavy thudding. The ground shook gently at first and then more violently. Small rocks on the floor nearby jumped about, and debris fell from the cave ceiling.

Finally, from the deepest recess of the cavern within a wide hole in the wall, the large head of a shadowy creature appeared. It slowly came out of the space like someone reluctantly rolling out of bed in the morning. The colossal life form took gentle steps toward Séya, who looked up into its glowing yellow-orange eyes and then bowed deeply as she often did when she had been away for long periods of time.

The creature also bowed, looking like an animal engaging in a stretch, and revealed itself in the light of the fire to be a large and beautiful, dark violet-colored dragon. When sitting upright, it was nearly as tall as a manor house. Bowing as it was, the dragon was roughly half that height.

"Up, child," the dragon said.

Séya slowly stood to find the dragon's head still bowed low. The eyes of the creature looked up, and the two embraced one another tightly. The rough hands were large enough to wrap around Séya's entire back, being careful of the claws. But the old woman wasn't worried and certainly wasn't afraid of dragon talons. In fact, she trusted her old friend with her life and felt the utmost comfort as the massive arms carefully enveloped her like a thoughtfully wrapped gift.

There was an unshakeable safety from the dangers and ills of the outside world in the care of a loving dragon. This was the very reason she was there.

"*Brrrr!* You are as chilled as ice!" the dragon exclaimed.

Séya chuckled and kissed her friend's smooth cheek. "Dearest Jessie."

"What news is there? Have you found more eggs?" asked the dragon.

"I'm afraid not," Séya said solemnly.

"I see," Jessie said. "Then what is it that brings you here at this hour? Another new pet?" Before Séya could respond, she went on. "I know they can be charming, but I cannot take one in, especially with five eggs waiting to hatch. I am sorry."

Séya gently touched Jessie's firm, scaled arm, and asked, "Would you take in a child then?"

The dragon's head tilted to the side.

"Come look."

Séya led her friend to the basket in the middle of the grass bed. The two of them cautiously peeked inside to observe the child, who was quietly looking up at both of them as the waterfalls persisted like a soothing melody that had no end.

4.

Neither Jessie nor Séya spoke. They just looked at the child, who kicked and moved around in the basket. The baby stayed mostly quiet, aside from the occasional murmurs.

"She's precious," said Jessie, whose voice was soft and sounded almost pained.

Séya looked at her friend, whose eyes were still on the baby. After all the years she'd known the dragon, she still never understood the magic Jessie possessed. Being a sorceress didn't make the mysteries any clearer to her.

"So, it is a girl," Séya said.

"Yes. Where did she come from?"

"I can't be sure," Séya replied. "I couldn't leave her where I found her."

"Hm, a Skylet," Jessie said. She took the name 'Skylet' from Séya's mind and thought it might be a good nickname for the child. Being a magical dragon, she could read thoughts. Sometimes, musings were so powerful that they seemed to burst from the mind of whoever held them.

Jessie smiled to herself but was hesitant in her response. "I couldn't, Séya. . ."

"Where else could she go? She wouldn't have much of

a life with me, you know?"

Jessie nodded.

"This was the safest place I could think of to bring her." Séya paused. "How many other dragons have you sheltered and protected? Surely a child would present less of a challenge!"

"And how many of them are here with me now?"

They both looked down and away from each other mournfully.

"How long has it been since you brought the last egg to me?"

Séya didn't answer.

"For all we know, the remaining eggs and I could be the only dragons left in the land, Séya," Jessie said. "That must be protected. The child would be better off with those like her."

"And what of me?" The old woman asked. "You protected me once."

Jessie slightly shuffled to the side as she turned away from both the baby and Séya. Looking over her shoulder, she met her friend's eyes. "That was different," she nodded. "You were not as vulnerable as she is. Not in the same way. You were. . . special."

"And this child is not?"

Jessie turned back to the basket and looked at the baby. The infant reached out her hands, and the dragon put a large middle finger into the vessel for the little one to grab with both of her tiny palms. Jessie used a finger that was curiously missing a talon to avoid accidentally hurting the child. "In her own way, she is."

Séya stepped underneath the dragon's wing and touched her arm. "Will you help me?"

Jessie slowly turned to face Séya and sighed deeply. "From the smell of things," she began, before turning a sideways glance at the baby. "This little Skylet needs a changing."

The two shared a chuckle.

"My talons are too sharp to even begin to try right now. So, my friend, will you help *me*?"

5.

The early morning hours were calm. Songs coming from the birds told her it was time to get moving and begin searching for some breakfast. A spirited thirteen years old, Skylet stalked the lush forest down the mountainside with a slingshot in one hand and two large rocks in the other.

The coarse, hairy straps from a coconut husk backpack that Séya had picked up on a trip tickled her bare shoulders as she moved, while the dark poof of thick curls on her head bounced against the back of her neck. She didn't feel like having to tie it up, so she let it stay open and free. The sun hadn't fully risen, but already she knew it would be a hot day and was glad she dressed for it.

The grass was both smooth and prickly under her feet, but she was used to the feeling and even preferred it to wearing shoes sometimes. Deeper she went until she found a tree resembling one from the juniper family, which had a large bunch of berries hanging from a high point.

Skylet readied her slingshot in an attempt to shoot the berries down, but before she could release the sling, a large shadow sped through the air like a sharp wind and snatched the berries up in one move.

"Hey! Cheater!" she yelled in protest.

A hearty laugh came from a large onyx-hued dragon and grew faint as he swiftly flew away from her. The powerful flapping of his wings created a gust of air that forced her back a bit.

She gave chase.

Unable to fly like the thief, Skylet found it challenging to keep her eyes on him as she ran, taking care not to trip over fallen branches and brush. She jumped over rocks and curved around trees, desperately trying to keep up.

The flying thief slowed down and dipped low enough that he was at her eye level. He whipped his large tail around to taunt her, and when she stopped to quickly fire her rocks, he successfully dodged them, laughing as he swerved away and returned to his higher position.

"I saw them first, Arca!"

"Too bad!" he shouted back. "Grow some wings if you don't like it!"

Skylet grunted loudly, continuing to follow him farther into the thick of the forest.

Arca made a sharp turn, but his large body quickly became entangled in a web of long, thick vines. He struggled to break free, and though he was strong, it wasn't enough. His arms, legs, and wings were wrapped up good.

Skylet laughed. "Give them to me!" She was triumphant, walking confidently toward him.

"Make me!" Arca yelled back as he continued to struggle.

Skylet took out a rock from the pouch she had on her hip and shot one up. It struck him in his exposed belly and bounced back as if she had flicked a pebble at him. Arca barely noticed.

When she bent down to pick up the stone intending to shoot it at his belly again, she heard a deep breath being drawn in loudly and suddenly felt an intense warmth against her back. She looked up and saw that Arca expelled fire from his mouth in an attempt to weaken the vines that trapped him.

Skylet quickly stepped to the side to avoid being hit by the thick and fiery falling vines.

With a mighty push of his wings, Arca was free. He laughed and flew away.

Skylet followed.

The dragon liked to show off, twisting and spiraling in the air. Skylet reached a boulder near the edge of a cliff on the mountain, which led down to a quiet valley. The girl positioned herself as if she were going to stand on top of it, but she didn't. Instead, she used the boulder to keep herself steady, preparing to fire a rock at Arca, who was in the process of flying upward in a looping fashion. The sky belonged to him.

Skylet took aim and breathed deeply as she waited for Arca to reach the bottom of his curl. When he closed the loop, looking behind him to see Skylet's position, Arca quickly shifted to the right in an attempt to dodge a flying stone, but Skylet hadn't released the sling just yet. Expecting another quick shot, he darted to the left, but she remained still and watched as he moved around.

He flew downward and grunted to himself, disappointed that she hadn't made a move. Arca decided that he would try to shake Skylet, so he positioned himself to fly straight toward her. They stared each other down.

Faster and faster, he flew at her like an arrow sprung from an archer's bow, but she didn't move. She stood still;

one eye closed, the other she used to aim through the slingshot. She saw his brown eyes narrow as he came closer, and when the moment was just right, she fired her shot.

The big rock struck Arca square in the eye. He yelped in pain, covering the injury with his large hands before crashing to the ground near where Skylet stood. She stepped off the boulder and approached Arca; whose body was contorted. His wings wrinkled from the tumble; his body nearly covered in dust.

Grumbling, he rubbed his eye as Skylet bent down and picked up the bunch of berries, putting them in her coconut husk backpack. "Take me to the spring Arca," she said calmly through a smile, picking a few twigs and loose leaves from her head of thick dark hair.

"Grrrr. . . For what?!" he spat.

"So we can wash the berries, silly."

"You could get there just as easily without me."

"Yes, but it's faster if you fly us there."

In a state of irritation, Arca whipped his head toward her, still rubbing his eye while wiping the dirt and dust from his onyx, leathery skin.

"I'll share the berries with you," she said.

"I don't want any of your berries."

"Come now, don't be a baby."

"I'm no baby!"

"Okay," Skylet shrugged. "Well, if you want some of these juicy berries, you know where I'll be."

Skylet began walking away. She turned to look at him on the ground expecting a response. Instead, there was silence. She looked off and continued on her way.

"Fine, get on." Arca bent over and allowed Skylet to get

on his back.

"Did you say something about victory being sweet like these berries?" she teased.

"Did you say something about me dropping you in the air?" Arca retorted.

The two shared a laugh; it was a memory that would echo in Skylet's mind long after that day.

6.

Skylet woke from her nap in the cave. The dream of a moment between she and Arca faded, giving way to the soothing sounds of a crackling fire and the waterfalls of the chamber. It was twilight; she could tell by how chilled the breeze felt against her face as it moved through the space, threatening to quiet the dancing flames from the fire. She pulled the thick blanket up over her shoulders to stay warm.

"Are you ready for your celebration dinner?" A voice from behind her asked.

Skylet turned around and saw Séya holding a large platter of food.

"Hi, Séya," said Skylet.

"We were afraid you would sleep through the whole day," Séya said. She placed the platter on a flat surface of a large tree trunk in front of Skylet, who sat up to take notice of the delicious treats in front of her. There were thinly sliced meats, salads, various pastries, fruits, and an assortment of nuts. It was a large meal, indeed.

"Everything you like from the Town's Heart is here," said Séya. "I've even found some new things for you to try!"

"Thank you Séya," Skylet replied, still trying to wake up. "Where is Jessie?"

"She'll be here any moment now," said Séya as she knelt in front of the girl. "How are you feeling, child? Did you have a good rest?"

Skylet nodded. "Mm-hm," she said, seeming unable to hold Séya's gaze for longer than a few moments.

"What is the matter?"

Skylet leaned back against a nearby log and stared beyond Séya and into the fire. The old woman moved closer to the girl, propped next to her, and released a deep sigh, seeming to know where Skylet's thoughts lay. "I miss Arca too," Séya said. "Four years now, can you believe it? The time seems to be flying along as swiftly as he once did around here." She chuckled. "Still, it seems like just moments ago, he hatched in this cave."

"He was in a dream I had," said Skylet.

"Was he now?"

"Yes. I was chasing him through the forest for a berry bunch." She paused. "I haven't thought about that day in a long time."

"Sounds to me like he's here in spirit," Séya said, wrapping her arms around Skylet, who leaned against the old woman's shoulder. They sat in silence, listening to the snapping fire against the subtle resonation of the waterfalls pouring into the cavern.

Just then, loud flapping could be heard, as if from the wings of a large bird. Clamorous rumbling followed.

"That'll be Jess," said Séya.

The closer the footsteps came, the more the ground trembled. Jessie entered from a large crater in the cave wall at the far end of the chamber.

"Hello, children," the dragon said.

The two ladies greeted Jessie.

"I hope you're hungry," Séya said. "There is enough food here to last for some time."

"For all three of us, Séya?"

"Seventeen years ago, I brought this child here," she said touching Skylet's cheek. "It is a special time."

"It is indeed," said Jessie. The dragon moved closer toward the two. She could feel sadness coming from Skylet. Jessie gently nudged her smooth, scaly nose against the girl's cheek, and Skylet reached up to embrace as much as she could of Jessie's large head.

"Would you care to share?" the dragon asked tentatively. "Only if you wish to."

Skylet leaned back to see the warmth in Jessie's face and nodded as the two of them closed their eyes, leaning toward each other.

The giant dragon hands gently cupped Skylet's head, and a pathway of sorts was opened. The memory of a mischievous young dragon and a girl chasing him presented itself to Jessie; it was as though she were living the event herself, watching from a distance. She could hear echoing laughter and allowed it to warm her heart before she removed herself from what she saw, coming back to the present moment in the cave. Jessie didn't want to feel as though she might be encroaching upon something so tender.

"Thank you, dear," she said, her voice was low. "I remember that day." Jessie exhaled, and Skylet was quiet.

The girl turned to look at the nearby fire as it burned.

"I have something special for you," said the dragon. She placed a gift wrapped in cloth and tied with rope onto the floor before Skylet. "Open it," she said.

Skylet untied the rope and unwrapped the cloth to find a hooded cloak made of dragon skin. It was the same dark violet color as Jessie. Skylet saw as she held up the mantle that it had a yellow-orange gem stitched into it: the color of Jessie's eyes.

"I made it myself. What do you think?"

"It's wonderful," Skylet said, her voice trembling. "Thank you."

"She didn't do it all by herself," Séya chimed in. "Of course, she had a bit of help from me. That was a great deal of shed skin to manage!"

Skylet chuckled. She hugged Séya tightly and kissed her cheek. "Thank you," she said.

"You are always welcome, child."

"I wanted you to have a piece of me," said the dragon. "With Séya's added touch, we hope you like it."

"I do," Skylet replied.

"We are always with you now," Jessie said. She moved in to hug Skylet. Séya joined, and Jessie wrapped her wings tightly around both of them.

"And so is Arca," Séya said, slightly waving her hand toward the ground. Something appeared on the floor in the middle of the huddle. "Look."

The three looked down and saw a pair of onyx-colored dragon skin shoes that doubled as boots. Leftover material from the cloak had been dyed to look nearly identical to what they remembered of Arca.

Skylet's eyes met the dragon's, and then she turned to Séya in surprise.

Jessie smiled. "To a wonderful seventeenth year."

7.

Jessie woke early the next morning well before the sun rose. She shuffled about the deep cavity within the mountain where she slept, trying to move as quietly as she could so as not to wake Skylet. Being that her size was as considerable as it was, some sound just could not be avoided. Her shuffling stopped as she tried to be still, listening to Skylet's breathing. Séya was also asleep nearby, having decided not to go back to her home after the celebration.

The dragon took a moment and set her eyes to the far end of the chasm, beyond a wide opening that looked out to the sky. She could see stars still twinkling in the distance, engaging in a lively conversation among each other. Daylight would soon arrive to chase away the night.

Someone stirring nearby brought her attention back to herself as she began to move again. It wasn't long before Skylet awoke and sat up. She could see the silhouette of the large dragon in motion. "What are you doing up so early, Jessie?" she asked in a hushed tone.

Jessie stopped moving and turned to look at Skylet, yellow-orange eyes glowing in the darkness. "I am excited," she said.

"Why?"

"Because I'm taking you somewhere special today," said the dragon.

"Where are we going?"

"To the sky."

"Really?!"

"Yes," the dragon giggled to herself. "Now go back to sleep."

Of course, it was almost impossible for Skylet to do that. She laid back down, but the racing of her mind kept her awake. Turning on her side, she smiled to herself in anticipation of the day.

***

Somewhere else in the mountains, a man rose to begin his morning. He stood up from his sleeping place on a smooth area of dirt and threw a thick, dark cloak made of dragon skin over his shoulders, clipping it together at the neck with a pin.

Looking out in the distance, he saw the rays of the sun cautiously creeping up over the mountaintops. He squinted his intense dark brown eyes and drew a deep breath before picking up a sheathed sword and unwrapping a necklace from its handle.

The man slung the weapon over his shoulder and put the necklace on, from which hung a large and thick shiny black talon, like one belonging to a giant eagle. He gently touched it, feeling the scratches and worn markings of its surface before letting it hang from his neck. Then he began to work his way down the long and arduous road of the mountain.

***

The air was brisk, but the morning sun felt warm against Skylet's face as she rode on Jessie's back far above the world below. To protect against the near-freezing temperature of the high altitude, she wore an insulated navy blue formfitting bodysuit that Séya had made, complete with a matching scarf which, along with her new cloak, were flowing in the wind.

Having left home before sunrise meant one less thing to worry about for Skylet. The idea of being noticed by the townspeople with a dragon was a terrifying one. She understood well the disdain the world seemed to have for not only dragons, but also for those like herself, whose skin was darker than most, and those like Séya who understood or wielded magical power.

Whenever they traveled, it was always either before dawn or after dusk and only when necessary. On other occasions, they journeyed during the midday, flying high enough that Jessie could be sure her size wouldn't be an issue. Sometimes, Séya would lead those excursions, having visited many places in her life. At other times, Skylet would stay with Arca and the other dragons under Jessie's care at the mountain.

Days that were heavily clouded offered more freedom to travel about, since the dragon could use the fog for cover, and fewer people seemed to be outside on days like that for fear of being caught in a potential storm.

They searched for food, or they would journey far beyond the bounds of Mysteya in search of eggs left behind in the Dragon Purge, a dark time that resulted in the near-extinction of dragonkind. Skylet and her siblings understood the stories all too well. For them, it would become very personal. But today was to be a happy day, and Skylet wanted to try her best to enjoy it with Jessie.

They tore through the air, Mysteya far behind them. Skylet turned around periodically as they moved farther away over the waters. She took note of the wide, lush valley behind the mountain cave they lived in and how small and insignificant it now seemed. The end of the valley was met by the redwood forest edge where Mysteya ended; it looked like nothing more than a spot of grass from her position. Skylet also saw other neighboring landmasses so small that they resembled tiny islands.

Whenever she traveled to new places with Jessie or when they passed a town she had never seen, she sometimes wondered what the people were like in those other lands. What sorts of foods did they eat? What were their customs? She would ask these questions until she came back to herself and settled on the thought that however they were, they would make little effort to welcome her or Jessie.

They flew high over the vastness of the water straight ahead to a place called Quentanan, where a tall mountain peak in the distance lay at its heart. Surrounded by trees of different types and shades that seemed endless, they all coexisted with each other in a manner that felt to Skylet like the kind of happy accident an artist embraces while creating a masterpiece.

With the exception of the mountain and the vast forests, there was nothing particularly remarkable about Quentanan. In fact, it was not so different from Mysteya.

According to the dragon, Quentanan had some of the juiciest citrus fruit around. It was her absolute favorite thing to eat, and Séya made a point to bring some from her many travels. It helped toughen dragon skin and strengthen fire breath, which was particularly important for hatchlings.

"There it is," Jessie said of the top of the mountain as they began their descent, flying over homes near the edge of Quentanan. "That's where we're going."

"It's so high," Skylet exclaimed, her eyes widening. "Higher than the mountains where our cave is!"

"That's why I call it The Sky," said the dragon. "There is no higher point around." They continued to soar until Jessie decided to have some fun. "Hang on," she said.

Skylet chuckled to herself and grabbed on to Jessie's large neck tighter, knowing what was coming next. The dragon swooped, dipped, and swirled in the air. They made silly noises and burst into laughter as any thoughts of hiding or surviving melted away. Their hearts felt as expansive as the empyreal sky they occupied, free in the purest of ways.

After a while, Jessie came in for a smooth landing at the wide, flat surface of the mountain. She allowed Skylet to slide down from her back as they gathered themselves.

"I forgot how much fun that was," said Skylet, catching her breath. "We haven't done that in a long time!"

"You didn't think I was so old that I couldn't move like that anymore, did you?" Jessie nudged Skylet with her wing.

"I guess you can!"

"Look," Jessie motioned for Skylet to turn around.

From where they stood, one could see nearly all of

Quentanan beyond the woods that surrounded them. Farther back, the large body of water they had crossed was visible, and beyond that, there was Mysteya, a mere blip in the distance.

"Wow," Skylet was mesmerized. "This is the most beautiful view I've ever seen! You can see everything from here!"

"It is quite breathtaking," the dragon said. "I used to come here often many years ago. Séya used to even come with me sometimes."

"How come you never brought me here before?"

The dragon turned away slightly. "Old wounds I didn't want to expose you to, I suppose."

Skylet looked down at Jessie's hands and remembered that the dragon was missing a talon from one of her middle fingers. "Is this where you lost it?"

Jessie nodded. "It is."

Skylet wrapped her arms around Jessie's forearm and looked up to face her. "What happened, Jessie?"

The dragon looked into Skylet's eyes lovingly before she responded. "We never really talked about it, have we?" Jessie asked rhetorically. "Well, Sky, you're old enough now to know."

Jessie got comfortable, and Skylet did likewise, looking at the dragon with anticipation.

"There are people you may meet," she began. "People who are less than agreeable. Many years ago, I crossed paths with one such person."

The moment of silence between them gave rise to the sounds of their quiet breathing, and the breeze whizzing around them. Jessie took a breath and continued her tale.

"There were hatchlings, long before you and Arca and

Beresay and Tithla. . ." she trailed off and looked out beyond the forests of Quentanan to the blip she saw as Mysteya in the distance. "Your brothers and sisters."

Skylet looked down and then turned her gaze beyond the mountain where they now sat.

"There were many others over the years; eight eggs under my care at once. Then, a Dragonhunter killed them. Stamped out their lives before they had a chance to take their first breath."

"Oh no," Skylet responded. "Where was Séya?"

"She was gone, searching for more eggs left behind during the Purge."

"People," Skylet spat. "They were destroying families."

"True," the dragon responded. "They were."

"What happened to the hunter?"

"I killed him," Jessie said in a matter of fact tone. She made no attempt to soften her response, turning to look Skylet in the eyes as she released those words.

Skylet's eyebrows rose, but she didn't move. She remained silent, waiting for more.

"We engaged in a lengthy battle that ended up here."

Skylet looked along Jessie's body and saw the evidence of old injuries with which she was all too familiar. Suddenly, the story of those scars had been spoken, laid bare for her to fully understand. She never thought to press for answers about where they came from, but now she knew.

"I thought it would be an easy strike for me," the dragon chuckled to herself. "He certainly provided a great challenge. Even up here, where I thought he would be out of his element, he was formidable."

"Don't your talons grow back when you sand them?" Skylet asked.

"Yes, but the hunter used a sword designed to prevent the quick healing we dragons possess."

"Well, I'm glad he's dead," Skylet said. "I might have killed him too."

The dragon touched Skylet's head with her large hand. "Don't judge him too harshly, dear," she said. "Yes, he committed an unspeakable act, but he only wanted to protect his people as I did mine. When you have something to protect, you could be likely to do anything. No matter what the cost."

They sat together, letting the sunlight warm their backs until a slight rumbling came from Skylet's stomach.

"I knew you would forget to pack the extra berries and nuts in your excitement, so I brought them," said the dragon, nodding toward the large bag that was attached to the end of her tail. "Time for breakfast."

8.

Marching swiftly through the thick of the temperate forest, the mysterious man moved with the grace of an animal comfortable in its habitat. He reached a small stream of water, next to which he found something that interested him. Kneeling, brushing away dead leaves and twigs, he touched the edges of what looked like the footprint of something very large. Something that didn't look like it was from the forest. He had been tracking the creature for some time before the trail went cold.

Whether the track belonged to a dragon or not, Oros's discovery was reinvigorating after a long period of no trace. He stood for a moment, examining the imprint, wondering which way the creature could have gone from there before making a guess. Just then, something rustled in the brush just beyond the stream, which brought Oros back to himself.

He looked up from the track, reaching over his shoulder for the hilt of his sword and holding steady until he could assess the threat. He dared not move, eyes narrowed, expecting to catch a glimpse of his enemy. Instead, a deer poked its head through the undergrowth, turning to acknowledge Oros's presence. He released the hilt of his blade and slowly lowered his hand. The deer's left ear twitched twice while staring at him before turning in the opposite direction and trotting off.

Oros exhaled deeply and hopped over the stream, advancing through the forest of oak and beech trees until he reached the margins of a bustling town.

He had arrived at the Scarlet Edge, so named for the brilliant red leaves of the scarlet oak trees that flanked his position. From great distances, the trees served as a marking point for travelers and passersby. When the sun was highest in the sky, the trees looked especially vibrant. It seemed like a gentle fire lighting the way in a dark tunnel. If lost, one needed only look to the Scarlet Edge to find their way again.

At the southernmost area of Mysteya, Oros took a moment to survey the land beyond him and decided to explore it.

He sauntered along the town border and entered as if he knew the area well, receiving awkward stares from some of the locals beginning their day, while others didn't seem to notice him. He walked along until he saw a tavern nearby. When he reached it, Oros stood outside, considering whether he should enter or continue moving. Then he heard a projected, gentle voice. "They haven't opened yet."

Oros turned to face the clean-shaven older man, dressed in an off white long-sleeved buttoned shirt underneath a brown vest. He had a full head of thick gray hair and deep lines on his face, each suggesting the many roads he had traveled, many lives he once lived. The old man, who was opening up his own place of business, gave Oros a slight nod.

"What is it that you sell here?" Oros asked the man.

"Medicinal herbs, teas, and such."

"And are you opening?"

"Just about. Come in and take a look if you like."

Oros accepted the man's invitation and followed him inside. The first room was essentially a large cube. There were many shelves from the floor to the ceiling, upon which sat jars of varying sizes full of herbs. At the far end of the room, Oros noticed a long, transparent curtain that covered a doorway leading to another cube of a room. No doubt, there were more herbs and teas back there.

"What is it that brings you out this way, stranger?" the man asked.

Oros took a second to respond as he was still perusing the space. "I've been on the trail of a dragon," he said. "Have you seen one around?"

The man chuckled at Oros's response. "Not for years," he said. "I do hear murmurs and whispers every now and again. No sightings, though. Unless you count the children who run around here wearing dragon skins."

Oros grabbed a few small jars of herbs, walking them up to the counter where the old man stood. "How much for these?" he asked.

"Three silver coins each."

As Oros went into the bag at his waist to pull out his pouch of coins, the man noticed the talon that hung around his neck. "Interesting necklace you have there," he said.

"Dragon talon," Oros said almost automatically as he rummaged through the bag, not making eye contact.

"And that cloak," said the man. "From a dragon?"

"It is," Oros responded. "The talon was claimed by my uncle, a great Dragonhunter from the old days."

"Fought many dragons then, did he?"

"He did," Oros replied. "This talon belonged to the one that killed him."

"I—I'm sorry," the man said.

There was a brief silence between the two. Oros paused as though trying to remember something he had forgotten.

"And what about the cloak if you don't mind my asking?"

"Made from the skin of a dragon I faced," Oros said matter-of-factly. The man wanted to know more but thought it best to stop there.

Oros paid for the herbs and placed them into his bag. He then bowed to the man, who nodded in acknowledgment. "My thanks. Be well," said Oros.

"Be well," the man replied. "Safe travels."

With that, Oros turned away and exited the place.

9.

Large bursts of fire flew from the top of the mountain. Skylet dodged them quickly and with great skill as they went every which way. She had her new hooded cloak to block the flames that Jessie shot toward her.

Dodgefire was a game Jessie played with her dragon children to help them learn about the fireproof qualities that their bodies possessed, and to teach them to control their fire breath. When Skylet was a child, she couldn't play without getting burned; she had to be supplied with a dragon skin blanket to keep her protected. After several years of playing the game, she was like a dragon in the way she moved.

"Ha!" Skylet shouted out as she spun around like a dancer, narrowly avoiding a fireball.

"Very good," Jessie said. "Now, let's see how you handle *this*!" The dragon sent a fireball considerably more massive than most at Skylet, who for a second stared at the swiftly approaching ball of flames with a determined smirk. She took a moment to appreciate the beauty, the poetry of the blaze in motion.

Instead of dodging as Jessie expected she would, Skylet used her cloak to deflect the fireball back toward the dragon, who was surprised at the action. The girl herself even seemed astonished by the almost instinctual move.

Jessie sent the ball back at Skylet with a swift brush of her large wing, and before long, the pair engaged in a volley.

Back and forth, the fireball went between them as they moved more acrobatically, both of them twisting and swerving, fully immersed in the game. Jessie somersaulted and used her whole body, including her head and tail, more than a few times to send the fireball back toward her opponent.

Watching the dragon in motion, Skylet was amazed at how agile and graceful she seemed for her considerable size. It was a sight she took for granted until moments like this; she was witnessing something spiritual to see a dragon fully in control and in tune with its body.

When it came time to end the volley, the dragon swiped the fireball upward toward the sky, where it eventually dissipated, signifying that she was ready for a break. "Phew!" The old dragon collapsed on the ground, smiling at Skylet. "I think I've earned a bit of rest!"

"That was fun," said Skylet out of breath, as she knelt in front of Jessie, so they were face to face.

"We'll need to head to the lake and clean up before we get back home," Jessie said. "Séya might have some things to say about us being dirty and sweaty before we eat any meals."

"Ha!" Skylet scoffed. "Séya gets plenty dirty too!"

Jessie chuckled. "Yes, she does."

***

Séya found herself crawling on her belly under a low ceiling of jagged rock. Her face and hands were sufficiently dirty, her clothes covered in mud. Yet, she crawled deeper through the damp cavern as if she were a creature of dark spaces. No stranger to this activity, she had been in similar situations over the years in her quest to preserve dragon life. Séya noticed something half shining in the darkness and continued to crawl toward it.

When she exited the tight cavern and found that she could now stand up, she opted to continue crawling, feeling comfortable against the cool surface. Moving closer to the object, Séya saw it was lit by the sunlight coming through holes in the cave walls. She realized that what she noticed was a dragon egg, which she had suspected, to begin with. It was surprising, particularly when considering that many months had passed since the last time she came across one that looked so promising.

Most eggs Séya encountered on her many searches had been destroyed before any baby dragons could take full shape. The new egg, was partially covered in mud, and it seemed to Séya that its mother hastily attempted to hide it from any potential threat.

The old woman gently picked up the egg, and before she could brush off some of the mud, she noticed a fracture and a piece of a dragon wing protruding through the surface of the shell. She sighed heavily then kissed the palm of her hand, placing it upon the egg, holding it there for a moment as she bowed her head and closed her eyes as if to say a prayer for the little one.

She stood that way in silence for a moment, before gently putting the egg back where she found it. Séya thought the unborn hatchling deserved a proper burial, so she carefully covered the cracked egg in the mud like a potter, lovingly crafting a cup, before she turned away and journeyed back the way she came.

***

Oros walked along a path that led away from the homes of the new town he was exploring. Though his expression was serious, his eyes were wide with wonder as he took in his surroundings.

He noticed immense, old maple trees and monarch butterflies that fluttered around nearby. There were richly colored tulips, balloon flowers, and lingonberry plants with luscious looking berries that caught his eye. He was surprised to come upon that particular plant as he was sure he hadn't heard its name since his uncle taught him about the medicinal uses of its leaves and berries as a boy.

He came across a group of children playing in a grassy yard who stopped to watch him. "You're a hunter," one boy called out.

Oros turned his attention away from the lingonberry plant to face the boy and only nodded.

"What is it you're after?" a girl asked.

Oros didn't answer. He only smiled at her slightly before continuing on the path. After a few more steps, he stopped and turned to the children, who he noticed were still watching him. "I'm looking for a dragon," he said to the girl.

"Like the one that burned a whole town?" another boy asked excitedly.

Oros paused and looked at him for a moment. Nearly everyone around knew the story, especially in Mysteya. It was legend.

Still, Oros was surprised anyone mentioned it. "And what would you know about that?" he asked the child quickly.

The boy was silent.

"Speak boy," he said firmly.

The young one was noticeably startled and stepped away slightly, as did the other children.

Oros took a breath and spoke more calmly. "Please."

The boy took a moment as if to sense whether or not the hunter would snap again. "Well, my mother told me," he began sheepishly. "That a long time ago, a dragon came to the old town of Selnes one night and burned it all down."

"Uh-huh," the little girl chimed in. "Everybody burned to death!"

"What happened to the dragon?" Oros asked.

It was a question no one really knew the answer to. Certainly, these children, who hadn't even been born yet, didn't know either. Still, he was curious about what they would say.

"The Dragonhunters killed him, my grandmother told me," said the last boy.

"I thought he died in his own fire," the first boy replied, perplexed.

"You both are wrong," said the girl. "The dragon was injured in a battle with the Dragonhunters and flew away to the stars."

Both boys looked at her. "Why would a dragon go to the stars?" asked the first boy. "Dragons fight!"

"Well, not when they are badly hurt," she said. "The stars are the safest place for dragons to go, of course."

They didn't know.

"Did *you* see the town burn down?" the first boy asked Oros, whose scruffy face contorted at the question.

"It was many years ago," he said, as he turned away from the children to continue his journey along the road. "I didn't see the town burn."

He moved on, straight ahead along the trail leading into the woods. The children stood and watched him for a minute before going back to their games.

10.

It was warm at Crescent Lake. Jessie and Skylet splashed themselves with water, freshening up from their earlier activities. The area was quiet and secluded, surrounded by bushes and many trees of oak, ash, and cottonwood. It was another special place they shared. The lake's grand crescent shape reminded Skylet of a shield. She felt safe, protected there.

"It will be time to meet Séya in town soon," said Jessie. "Are you ready to continue your fun?"

"I am," she said excitedly. Then her face became somber.

Jessie knew what was going through Skylet's mind. "I wish I could join you both, too," said the dragon.

Skylet looked down at her reflection in the water.

"An entire town could do great damage to a well-meaning dragon."

"I know," replied Skylet.

They sat in the lake for a while longer, talking of trivial things until Jessie got out and made ready to leave. "I will see you when you get back. Have a pleasant time with Séya," the dragon said.

Skylet raced to the dragon and hugged her.

"And be sure you're all dry before you head into town or else—"

"I know," Skylet chimed in, kissing the dragon's bowed head. "See you."

"All right," said Jessie, pulling out a small glass jar containing a clear liquid from the bag tied to her tail. "Stand aside, dear."

Skylet stepped back.

The dragon tossed the jar above her head and quickly shot a fire dart at it, causing it to pop. The clear liquid reacted to the fire, creating a mist that began to cover the dragon, and making parts of her invisible.

Séya had concocted a potion that was a quick and very temporary solution to the potential issue of Jessie being seen should she have to travel in the middle of the day. It wouldn't last very long, so the dragon had to move quickly enough that by the time she reached a certain altitude, she would be so high she could never be made out by anyone happening to glance toward the sky.

Just before Jessie was fully covered, she nodded her partially visible head toward Skylet, and soon, she was totally invisible. With tremendous flaps of her large wings, Jessie took off straight into the air, water droplets spattering everywhere. Small trees and bushes flailed around in her wake.

Skylet looked up, listening to the whooshing of the dragon's wings, trying to guess the position she might be in. She watched for a while longer before finding a nice large boulder to lean against in order to be dried by the sun, warming her bronzed skin.

When she was dry enough to get dressed, she changed

into more comfortable clothes and headed into town, turning back once to admire how the sunlight bounced off the surface of the lake water.

Moving through the bushes and beyond the brush, she soon found herself deep in the forest, walking along until she found a pathway partially obstructed by leaves and twigs. The bustling sounds of the town in the distance told her she was going in the right direction. It had been so long since she last came to the lake with Jessie and Séya that she had almost forgotten how to find the different pathways that led to the Town's Heart.

Arca was with them the last time they all came and played at the lake with the other dragon children. The memory of that time was a tender spot in Skylet's heart now that Arca and her other siblings were gone. It was something she tried not to think about.

Shuffling ahead brought her back to the present moment as she traversed the trail. She noticed a man in the distance through the limbs of the trees, which partially obscured her vision. Oros walked with purpose, and his face was solemn. He was hunched over, scowling at the ground as if he were a bloodhound on the hunt. Skylet could hear jingling with each step he took. Coins? Keys? She wondered what the man carried that made the sounds.

As he came closer to her, she noticed he wore a cloak of dragon skin, which stirred something inside her. She felt a wave of heat in her stomach, but suppressed the feeling and kept moving, intent on reaching her destination. It wasn't only that the man was wearing dragon skin that elicited a discomfort within her. It was that the cloak was of an onyx color, which made her afraid. She only ever knew one dragon with that color skin. Her brother Arca, and he was gone.

Closer and closer, the two came to one another until they passed each other without so much as a nod or gesture. They hadn't gotten two steps beyond the other before Oros turned to speak. "Pardon me, miss," he said, looking at the ground. His voice was gravelly but clear and focused. "I'm looking for a large creature."

Skylet didn't respond immediately. She looked at the ground and then her eyes worked their way to his boots up to his belt and finally his cloak. She couldn't pull away from the sight. "I'm not sure how I can help you, sir," she said in an even-tempered tone, trying to keep from sounding nervous.

"I'm looking for a dragon. A massive one," he said. "Might you have seen one around here?"

Skylet's heart sank. She had been with Jessie all morning, and as far as she knew, there were no other dragons around. She blinked and looked at his rough face, tanned from the heat of dragon fire, noticing that his eyes were scanning her. A sight which made her uncomfortable enough to hold on to her bag tighter and gingerly take a step back. "I'm sorry," she said. "I don't think there are any dragons around here." She took another step back.

Oros calmly looked at Skylet's face, which was just as serious as his. "That is mighty nice dragon skin you have about you," he said, referring to her garments. "Might I ask how came you by it?"

"My mother," she said quickly. Skylet felt herself losing her composure.

"I see," said Oros. He stepped in for a closer look at her cloak and spotted fresh burn marks on it. He also noticed something else: a smell coming from Skylet that had a particular charred scent, mixed with a fleshy quality typically associated with dragons. It was a smell he knew well. Oros stood more upright now; a confidence slowly built within him.

Skylet took another, more purposeful step back.

"Are you certain you haven't seen a dragon around here?" he asked. "Seems to me like you could have gotten into a disagreement with one." He chuckled to himself.

"I'm very sorry, sir," she said. "I have seen no dragon."

The two looked dead at each other's faces, their eyes locked in a staring match.

Skylet fought off the overwhelming urge to turn and run. "I must be off now," she said. "I hope you find the one you are searching for."

She slightly bowed, and Oros did likewise. "Sorry to have troubled you," he said. "Do be well."

"And you, sir."

The girl didn't waste a moment. She quickly turned and continued on her way, while Oros stood and watched as Skylet's pace quickened. He pondered on the dragon articles she wore, and as he did, his mind wandered to the smell he noticed earlier. It took him back to when he was a boy, returning home to find his town destroyed by dragon fire. It had a scent distinct from other kinds of fire.

His training as a Dragonhunter also further underscored what he suspected: the girl was lying. Oros slowly began to walk along the trail and continued to think on how he might find the dragon about which he was certain she knew.

II.

After a long while of walking in haste, Skylet reached the Town's Heart of Mysteya. Located at the very center, it was where the most action took place. Teeming with people moving every which way, they carried on spirited and exciting conversation. Everything from the markets to the tailoring shops was seemingly overwhelmed with patrons, as though a festival or some other event was in town. But it was just another day.

As Skylet made her way through the crowds, she could barely keep from turning to see if she had been followed. She was supposed to meet Séya at an old well near the edge of where the Town's Heart ended but was too wrapped up in her thoughts to sit and wait there. She couldn't shake the notion of the mysterious man she encountered on the trail and wondered who he was. Why was he searching for Jessie? She concluded that he meant ill for the only living dragon she knew and was anxious to tell Séya what had happened.

Skylet kept walking past the well and ended up at Séya's home, where she sat on the wooden steps and waited. She couldn't be certain how long she was there, but the sun had slightly moved since she first arrived at the doorstep.

After some time, Séya came home very dirty and out of breath. "Ah, there you are!" she exclaimed. "Why on earth weren't you at the well?"

Skylet shrugged her shoulders and looked up at Séya with a forced smile.

"Well, I'm glad you're here! I'll get cleaned up and then we'll be off!" Séya was excited; she quickly breezed past Skylet up the stairs to her door and opened it.

"Phew!" Séya exhaled as she began taking off articles of dirty clothes and tossing them in a pile near her bedroom. "Feel free to help yourself to any sort of snack you like before we leave, dear."

Tossing her bag down, Skylet plopped herself onto one of the red cushioned armchairs nearest the small oak table in the center of the living room and sighed heavily.

"Did you have a good time this morning with Jessie?" Séya asked as she moved about.

"I did," Skylet said in a manner that seemed off to Séya.

"You don't sound like it," the old woman responded through a smile, but she didn't stop moving.

"I saw a man, Séya," Skylet began.

"You did? Well, was he handsome?" Séya chuckled a bit.

"He wore dragon skin." Skylet shuddered at the thought of the man's cloak.

Séya stopped undressing herself and became serious. The atmosphere in the room changed. Séya, half dressed, slowly took a seat in the chair across from Skylet and looked on intently, waiting to hear more.

"I was on my way in to meet you and I saw that his cloak reminded me of Arca," she said.

Séya looked down at the table. "Did he have a sword?" she asked.

"I think he did," replied Skylet. "He was looking for a dragon." She looked at Séya who sighed.

"He was a hunter," the old woman said. "He's looking for Jessie."

"Why?"

Séya got up and walked to a dresser in the corner of the room behind Skylet. She made sure the window curtains were completely closed before opening a drawer and dug deep to remove a small wooden box before coming back to the chair and sitting down. Skylet looked on in anticipation as Séya opened the box and removed a small clear vial with a silver band around it. It was full of a plum-colored liquid. She handed it to Skylet, who began examining it.

"Do you know what this is?" Séya asked.

"Blood?"

"Dragon's Blood," said Séya. "This, I think, is why the hunter is after Jessie."

"Why do you have this?" she looked up at Séya.

"Jessie gave it to me," the old woman responded. "Many years ago. In case I ever needed it."

Skylet looked back at the vial.

"In the old days, Dragonhunters were more or less honorable and acted as town protectors to some extent," Séya said. "Before the Sentinels. Dragons were only killed if they fatally attacked other people." She continued. "Then it was discovered, rather by accident, that the blood of a dragon could heal wounds sustained in battle. This was the beginning of the long extinction for dragonkind. The Dragon Purge."

Séya spoke of how this knowledge of the blood's power spread to armies of men who soon began killing dragons for no other reason than to collect the blood and harvest it. Soldiers would turn on each other for the precious resource.

At some point, Skylet stopped shaking and allowed Séya's words to enter her ears. As she took in the horrors being described to her, she felt something brimming inside that wasn't there before. It was a heat that had quickly made itself known to her as deep anger. She experienced enough from being around dragons most of her life to understand the harshness dealt to dragonkind, and she had almost always felt fear and distrust of other humans who were not Séya. Now though, she was learning more than she had ever known. What was once distrust and fear now turned into unbridled hate.

"Jessie told me about a hunter she killed," Skylet said. "He cut off her talon."

"Do you know why that talon has never grown back?" Séya asked.

Skylet shook her head. "Jessie said something about a sword that stops dragon healing."

"Moonbeam Metal," Séya said.

"Moonbeam Metal? What's so special about it?"

"The legend is that a blacksmith made a sword in the dark of night by only the light of a full moon for the first town protector, long before there were any Dragonhunters. The moonlight infused the metal with power. So, it was discovered later, that anything made from this metal could stop the natural healing and regenerative abilities of a dragon. Moonbeam Metal weapons have been the mark of Dragonhunters ever since."

Skylet sat quietly for a moment and remembered the scars she saw on Jessie's body. It all made sense. She thought back to the hunter she encountered in the woods and the cloak he wore, reminding her of Arca. Tears began to form in her eyes as she collected herself enough to respond. "We have to tell Jessie," she said, but she sounded distant Séya noticed.

"Dear child, I'm sorry to have upset you." Séya put on a thick shirt nearby and pulled her seat near Skylet, putting an arm around her.

"Arca is dead," Skylet spat out into the space of the small room, which suddenly felt vast to her with only she and Séya in the middle of it. "That man killed him."

Séya looked down, her eyes darting around different parts of the fuzzy brown rug beneath them. Rather than speak, she thought it best to stay silent and let Skylet feel the emotions.

The girl looked at her boots and suddenly felt moved to do something for her brother. She slowly stood up and walked to the window near the front door. "I'm going home," she said.

Séya didn't respond. She stood up and completed dressing herself. When she put on her robes, she walked to the front door, opening it. "Then let us go," she said solemnly.

The two of them moved to the entrance, Skylet stepping out first. Séya followed and closed the door behind her as the two headed back to the mountain where Jessie rested.

12.

Oros was in the thick of the woods, thinking about the young lady in the dragon skin. His mind swirled with thoughts on what the beast looked like and how large it might be. The idea of what a battle would be like against it occurred to him, and he imagined himself victorious. The more he pondered on the dragon, the more curious he became about Skylet.

The particular color of her cloak struck him in a way he couldn't quite place. It seemed familiar to him, but he couldn't remember exactly where he had seen it. It was a unique dark violet color that was as rich as blood, and it stirred a feeling within him that wasn't a happy one.

Oros stopped when he reached an oak tree, leaning against it to rest for a moment. As he sat, he heard the soothing sounds of water kissing the lake edge, which was a refreshing thought since he was beginning to feel very hot on his trek.

He followed the sound until he reached Crescent Lake, kneeling over it to splash the cool water in his face. Oros stood up to take a breath as he surveyed the area, noticing the bushes, cottonwood, ash, and oak trees surrounding him. He began to take slow steps around the perimeter of the lake, listening to the water and feeling the occasional soft breeze.

The hunter moved along until he noticed something in the dirt near a group of large rock formations. It had a slightly reflective quality, like a glossy piece of parchment. The thin object was a dark violet color. Kneeling, Oros picked it up and rubbed it between his fingers, looking at it closely and examining its texture. He knew instantly that what he held in his hand was unmistakably a scale from a dragon. Oros turned and looked beyond the lake in the direction he had come. His thoughts took him back to Skylet once more.

***

Skylet and Séya moved through the forest and approached the foot of the mountain. The hike had been mostly silent between the two of them. Séya didn't know what to say after a while, but she thought she might try engaging Skylet once more before they saw Jessie. "You're awfully quiet, dear," she said. "Whatever are you thin-king?" Their pace quickened together as they moved along the hill that led up the mountain.

"Nothing," replied Skylet. She sounded irritated, deep within her thoughts.

"Listen, I am worried too," Séya said in an attempt to calm Skylet's nerves. "It'll be okay when we talk to Jess."

"All right," replied Skylet, in a detached manner. There was an anxiousness in her tone that Séya could feel.

Eventually, they reached the inside of the mountain and Jessie was called. "Jessie!" cried Skylet. She didn't want to wait for a response so she climbed up to the cave hole where Jessie slept.

The old dragon was just getting up to hear what all the fuss was about. "What is it?" asked Jessie, but something within the girl gave her the answer.

Skylet's emotions and thoughts spoke so loudly that it was impossible for the dragon not to read and feel. Jessie could almost see Skylet's worries weighing on her like a large backpack that was too heavy. For a moment in the dim light of the cave, Skylet looked older, her face stone serious, devoid of all traces of the joy she was bursting with just hours earlier. More like a concerned parent than the free-spirited young woman she was.

Still, Skylet was carrying the weight well enough, but she was looking for help managing it, and Jessie felt it all. The dragon sighed and waited for Skylet to respond.

"I saw a man in the woods on my way to meet Séya," she said out of breath.

"And you think this hunter is looking for me?" Jessie asked.

"He wore a cloak made from the skin of a dragon," Skylet shot back. "He killed Arca. I know it!"

Jessie looked down in silence. "Sky—" began the dragon.

"Did you know what happened to him?" Skylet asked quickly.

"I didn't."

"You didn't?" Skylet's breathing was becoming more audible. "You know what else you didn't do?"

"Skylet—" Jessie's voice was harder.

"You didn't stop him from leaving! You could have saved him!" Skylet shouted.

Séya was just coming into the cave hole.

"Arca's spirit was fierce," Jessie said. "He was too wild to be held back. . ."

"You didn't care enough to go and find him!"

Séya gasped in surprise. "*Skylet!*" she said breathily.

"I did care," Jessie said, slowly turning her large head to face Skylet. Her yellow-orange eyes slightly glowed in the dark hole of the cave. It was unsettling to the girl, who took a half step back. In the shadows of the deep crevasse, she couldn't make out Jessie's facial features, but she could feel a scowl. Still, Skylet didn't turn away.

"I raised Arca from a hatchling, as I have raised you," said the dragon. "I loved him too. He just couldn't wait one day. You remember."

"She had to stay with you, dear," Séya chimed in softly, gently touching Skylet's shoulder. "She couldn't risk getting captured or killed with you here all alone."

Skylet began to break down. Tears streamed from her eyes and rolled down her cheeks.

Jessie was quiet.

"Well," said Skylet through sniffling, "What are we going to do now that the hunter is looking for you?"

"Should he ever find me, we will deal with it then."

Skylet scoffed. "That is foolish. He saw my cloak and my boots! What if he calls other hunters to search for you?"

"Then we will deal with that," Jessie said, looking straight at Skylet, who shook her head fiercely. "Let's not worry about any of that until we have to."

Skylet paused and took a deep breath before turning swiftly to leave the cave hole, slipping away from Séya's touch.

"Skylet," said the old woman, but there was no response.

The girl had climbed down the rocky wall and stormed out of the cave.

13.

The silence between Jessie and Séya was hard for the sorceress to endure. The dragon's yellow-orange eyes slowly moved to Séya, who was staring at the dark ground before she looked up and found the eyes of her old friend. "She's just a little shaken, that's all," said Séya. "If I am truthful, I am worried too."

"I am not," said the dragon.

Séya came closer to Jessie and stroked the side of her large face. "You did what was best for her. You know that. If something had happened to you as well. . ."

"Sometimes I wonder about my choices."

"I know," replied Séya.

The dragon looked down at the ground.

"Jessie, you made the best decision for her. Any hatchling needs a dragon mother who knows the histories in order to pass them down."

"I kept a lot of that history hidden from her."

"Of course you did," Séya said. "She would not have been able to handle it all before."

The silence between the two returned. Séya took a moment before she spoke again. "I will go and see after her. Then we'll all talk."

"I think you should let her have her time right now," Jessie said.

"I won't be very long." Séya turned and left the crevasse.

***

Walking through the low hanging brush and pine trees along the mountainside, Skylet kicked and swore to herself. She couldn't understand Jessie's apparent ease about what she had just shared, wondering if they should all leave or if they should remain in hiding.

In thinking more about it, she did take some comfort in the fact that the cave was well hidden, having lived there her whole life without a single outsider ever stumbling upon it. Then again, she had never seen another person in dragon skin clothing before either. Anything could happen now, she thought. She couldn't let herself be fully at ease.

Skylet stopped and leaned against a pine tree, allowing herself to slide down to the ground as she wrestled with her feelings. The only dragon that she knew was alive had a hunter looking for her, which didn't mean anything good as far as Skylet could tell. She asked herself why she was so angry with Jessie but never came to an answer.

Looking at her left knee, she thought back to when she broke her leg in a nasty fall on the last night she had seen her brother four years before. Skylet, Arca, and Jessie's other dragon children flew to a forest on the side of a mountain at the edge of Mysteya, which bordered a neighboring town. The forest was one they had traveled to often on summer nights when they wanted to play games or tell scary stories around the campfires that Skylet made.

She was always proud of the fires she built with sticks from the forest. Séya taught her how, as a child, and Skylet reveled in reminding the others that she didn't have to be born a dragon to make fire.

The forest was a place they all thought was secret and safe, and it was. Until it wasn't anymore. Sitting at the tree, Skylet saw it all as clear as if it were happening in front of her.

Arca put out the campfire with his hands as they all prepared to go back home. Then without warning, a group of soldiers surprised them, bursting through the bushes. They had apparently been watching the forest for months when whispers began moving around that dragons had frequented the area. It was a planned attack.

The dragons that tried to fly away were shot down with arrows and captured in large nets lined with Moonbeam Metal so that any wounds they had wouldn't heal.

Skylet and Arca tried to fly away, but the girl slipped off of his back in the midst of dodging arrows and blades, falling into the woods many feet below. She snapped her leg against the thick branch of a tree, landing on a small area of rocks and grass.

Arca swooped in through the trees and carefully picked her up as quickly as he could, pushing up from his hind legs with all his force, holding her in his arms as he flew up out of the forest.

After getting back home, Arca and Jessie argued over what had happened and about whether or not Arca should be allowed to go and search for the other dragons. "I'm going back for them," Arca said firmly.

"You will not," the dragon replied. "Stay with Skylet and help tend to that leg."

"No!" he exclaimed.

"Arca, you need to keep your head about you," the elder dragon said. "We are all that's left. If you should be captured or worse. . ." she trailed off and shook her head. "I will search for them. I can sense them in ways that you cannot."

"I don't care about that," he spat. "I will find them."

Arca turned away from her and made ready to leave, moving toward an exit in the cave, wings poised to take him to the sky.

He wouldn't get very far before Jessie jumped in front of him with a speed that he hadn't known she possessed. He blinked in astonishment, staying himself. It became clear to Arca that Jessie probably had many other tricks she never really displayed.

Skylet sat in a corner of the cave, with tears in her eyes, watching the two of them deliver hard stares toward each other. Arca let out a sigh and relaxed himself, turning away from Jessie to walk toward Skylet.

"She needs you Arca," the dragon said, her body now slightly less tense. "I will go."

"Fine," he responded in a tone that smacked of indifference to Skylet.

When Arca reached her, he lowered himself to her level and put his head against hers, gently placing his large hands over her small ones as she held her tightly wrapped leg.

Jessie watched as the two met each other's gaze.

Skylet slowly shook her head as if to tell him not to leave, but she could feel it. Even in that moment of closeness between them, Arca had already gone.

As Jessie turned away from them, preparing to leave

the cave, a large shadow sped past her toward a different exit. Jessie cursed herself for having missed Arca's thought to try and escape. She sensed too much of his frustration to catch anything else in his mind.

Without thinking, she reached out and grabbed his tail. Holding tightly, she forcefully brought him to the ground.

Skylet could feel the vibration of the trembling floor from the hands and feet of the heavy dragons now engaged in a struggle.

Arca moved and twisted about, flipping his tail and flapping his wings wildly in an attempt to break free of Jessie's grip. Nothing worked until he brought his arms, legs, and wings inward before pushing himself upward from his belly.

He quickly tucked his head down, forming himself into a ball to roll forward.

Jessie lost her grip of Arca's tail, and as he faced her, his body was low as though he prepared to defend himself.

Before Jessie could move toward him, Arca quickly shot out a burst of fire at her. She used her wings to block the blast, which pushed her back slightly before dissipating into a puff of smoke.

"ARCA!" Skylet exclaimed.

He didn't respond or look away from Jessie. The two dragons stared at each other, out of breath. They spoke no words.

Jessie was noticeably shaken, but her look remained serious.

Arca now stood up straighter, though he too seemed remorseful of his actions.

Breathing fire at another dragon intentionally was

considered a tremendous sign of disrespect. It almost always meant that a fight would ensue. But there was no further struggle between them.

Jessie let out a sigh, fighting back her emotions, and slowly stood up straighter to meet Arca.

It was customary for dragon children to stand up straight when they reached adulthood as a sign that they were ready to leave home. The parent who acknowledged this would return the action. While Arca was not quite an adult yet, Jessie could see that she would not be able to stop him without hurting him. She had to let him go.

Arca could no longer hold Jessie's gaze. He looked to Skylet at the far end of the cave space. She met his eye, tears streaming down her face, searching herself for something to say to him, but nothing came.

Arca's eyes met the floor, and he quickly turned away, jetting off beyond the girl's line of sight. His flapping wings could be heard in the distance, while the waterfalls running through the cavern and crackling fire from wall lanterns seemed loud among the silence.

Jessie became so overcome with emotion that she screamed at the chamber ceiling; the harsh sound reverberating off the walls, rumbling the ground. She couldn't leave Skylet with a broken leg all by herself.

When Jessie calmed down, she walked over to comfort the girl who sat on the cave floor in tears, managing a tremendous amount of pain. The dragon looked up through a hole in the cave ceiling and began to brood.

As Skylet came back to the present moment, she sat with her thoughts on that night and realized that she was angrier with herself than she was with Jessie, feeling that if she had spoken up and said more, maybe Arca would have stayed. Now, as far as she knew, Jessie was in danger.

Skylet became lost deep in the notion of Jessie's safety when she heard Séya calling her name in the distance. She didn't move; she just sat there with her back against the tree, holding her face in her hands, sobbing harder.

"Skylet!" Séya called out. She was getting closer.

Skylet remained where she sat, wiping her eyes. She looked to her right, where she saw the old woman approaching. Still, she sat there looking defeated.

Séya got within feet of Skylet when suddenly a small white bag the size of an acorn dropped between them and exploded into a thick white mist. It came from seemingly nowhere and spread through the area in seconds.

Startled, Skylet quickly stood up and attempted to run toward Séya. "Séya!" She cried, hearing quick shuffling behind her.

She turned around, and before she knew it, she was overcome by a large figure whose face was obscured, wrapped in a dark mask.

Skylet struggled, kicked, and screamed, but she couldn't break free.

Séya could only partially see the outlining of the two bodies engaged in the struggle through the fog. She ran deeper into it to break the girl away. "Skylet! I'm coming!"

The smog was so thick that Séya was quickly beginning to lose perspective, her sense of direction failing. She stopped and crouched her body like a cat preparing to pounce on an unsuspecting mouse. Then she closed her eyes and gently waved her hands in a circular motion. Right hand, left hand, one after the other she moved as if she were engaging in a dance.

Soon the fog began to clear up from the inside out. She

opened her eyes to see Skylet trying to get free.

The figure pulled something from a pouch on his belt and quickly shoved it in Skylet's face. The struggle became more intense momentarily and then the girl stopped moving.

"Get back!" Séya shouted. "Release her!" She started running again when she saw the man put a black sack over Skylet's head and pick her up over his shoulder. "Release her *now!*"

"Back, witch!" the figure spat. He tossed a second small white bag just in front of Séya. It hit the ground, exploding into another wall of thick white fog.

She jumped back slightly and covered her eyes.

"I want no part of you," he said. "Stay where you are."

"Like hell," Séya said, almost to herself. She ran as fast as her aging body would allow, but she could no longer see anything. Cursing to herself in frustration, she raised her right hand and brought it down with a force that made a loud swooshing sound, accompanied by her audible grunt. It took a great deal of energy, and she dropped to one knee, nearly breathless. The fog cleared away almost instantly as if she had a giant hand to brush the smoke away in one swoop.

There was no trace of the man or Skylet. Séya found herself alone. "Oh," she said to herself under her breath. She sat, trying to understand what happened until something glistening in the distance caught her attention. Séya's eyes narrowed to get a better view. She crawled closer, gingerly collecting the item and holding it in her hand. It was the small yellow-orange gem from Skylet's dragon skinned mantle that came off during the struggle. Suddenly Séya could not contain her emotions, and tears trailed down her face freely.

Back at the cave, Jessie sat coiled in a resting position alone with her thoughts. She realized that Séya had been gone for longer than expected and began to worry that maybe Skylet had run off. The dragon got up from her spot and began to make her way out of the crevasse. The closer she came to the cave opening, the more she noticed the sounds of someone crying. Something felt particularly urgent about the cries and without thinking, she composed herself then flew off in a flash.

14.

Séya's face flushed, wet with tears of despair and anger. She stayed on her knees, staring dejectedly into the yellow-orange pin as if it would make Skylet appear next to her. The girl didn't appear. But a large shadow did.

Leaves and dirt suddenly blew around Séya as if strewn about by great winds. Jessie landed to find Séya on her knees with her head down. The dragon moved slowly toward her friend, and when she was close enough, she leaned her head over, just above Séya's.

The old woman put her right hand up and held it open to Jessie, revealing the pin. The dragon's eyes glossed over, as if she were looking at nothing.

Séya turned and looked up at Jessie, whose eyes she met. The two spoke no words to each other.

***

The first sense that came to Skylet was that of smell. The salt in the air was potent. The next sense she regained was that of sound. Muffled though it was, she could hear what she knew to be the splashing of water around her. The breeze was crisp against her skin, and the sun's rays were intensely warm, creating a strange sensation of cool heat. She couldn't move but felt as though she were being rocked back and forth in a cradle like a baby. No matter how she tried, she couldn't open her eyes. It seemed to her that she had been asleep for much longer than she had ever slept. Even if she could open her eyes, there was still the matter of the black sack, which covered her face.

She was remotely aware of her surroundings and had a fleeting thought that she might be on a boat, but soon she blacked out and knew nothing.

When she became mindful of herself next, she was being carried over the shoulder of a big man. Still, she couldn't see anything because her eyes were too heavy for her to open. It was not comfortable at all for her, being unable to move, feeling the shoulder dig into her stomach.

She heard the muted sound of jingling items, which made her mind go back to when she came across the Dragonhunter in the forest. She saw Arca's face looking at her warmly before it faded into nothingness, replaced by a pang of sadness in her chest. She couldn't harp on that for too long, as she soon blacked out again.

It was on a small cot that Skylet came to, feeling her brow damp with sweat. Finally, she was able to slowly open her eyes—only to discover her vision was blurry. The light of day, pouring in through a window in the small room, made her eyes sore. Feeling weak, she trembled with each move. Her stomach rumbled, but she gave in to the frailty she felt and resolved to rest until the distant speech of a man in the corner of the room startled her. "When you are able to move more easily," the voice said, "be sure to eat."

In the center of a low, long table of oak wood, there

was a large plate of fruit, everything ranging from strawberries to sliced melons, the scent of which gave the room an aromatic quality. Next to the plate sat a large metal cup of water.

"Your body is no doubt in need of sustenance."

"I. . . I can't see. Where are you?" Skylet asked. Her voice was hoarse, and her body was tense.

There was a beat of silence with no answer from the voice.

"Three days have passed," he said finally. "You should eat."

"Three *days*?" Skylet's voice cracked. "Where is Séya? Where are we?"

"Eat," said the man. "The delirium will wear off sooner." He stood up and walked toward the door, leaving her alone.

Skylet groaned as she tried to position herself to sit up on the cot. Her vision was still blurry enough that she could barely make out the shapes in the stone room. When she reached up to rub her eyes, she struggled, her arms felt like heavy sacks.

Suddenly, Skylet had the idea to get on her feet in an effort to find answers to her questions. She didn't get very far at all, standing halfway upright before her knees buckled beneath her. She fell, knocking other items off of the table onto the cool floor with her.

Skylet groaned again. Managing to roll herself over onto her back, she shut her eyes, blacking out once more.

15.

The cave was quiet save for the constant sound of the waterfalls. In the three days since Skylet's disappearance, Jessie and Séya sat across from one another in the grass patch of the cave's central area. Heads bowed, eyes closed, Séya's small hands placed inside Jessie's large ones. They looked as though they were praying, but they were doing something else that was no less spiritual.

Engaged in a silent conversation, they tried what they could, hoping to locate Skylet. Séya whispered words and phrases under her breath as a cool breeze swept through the cave. The fire from the torches along the walls that surrounded them was small and quiet at first. Then the draft became so strong that the flames nearly blew out. Though their eyes were closed, in the darkness, they could see flashes of light.

The flashes turned into images of the cave, the mountain, and the area surrounding it outside. By some magic she possessed, Jessie made it possible for the two of them to share Séya's memory of the day Skylet disappeared. The dragon was able to see through Séya's eyes everything that happened. She lived each moment, felt each step Séya took, and each emotion Séya felt.

Day by day, they studied the memory in an attempt to see where Skylet might have gone. Jessie was able to put herself in the moment and somehow scan the area, but she could only go so far before the boundaries of the memory restricted her.

The dragon was worried, but after three days, she could scarcely feel it, becoming more numb than anything else. When it got late at night, Séya opted not to go to her home in town and instead would go to sleep nearby while the dragon tried to track Skylet on her own without the memory. More specifically, she attempted to detect the cloak, which came from her skin.

Jessie sat and stayed up for hours, using her mental magic to try and discover any clue. She was certain that figuring out Skylet's location was possible but hadn't had any luck so far.

After a long while, Séya was having trouble staying awake. "I suppose I'll head off to sleep," she said. "Good night."

"Good night," Jessie replied. The dragon looked up to the cave ceiling, her eyes wandering toward a hole to the right, which was open to a starry night sky. It reminded her of when Séya brought home baby Skylet those many years ago, a memory she saw as clearly as anything right in front of her.

Jessie drew a deep breath and curled halfway into a coil. But she did not sleep that night.

16.

Skylet opened her eyes to find that she had slept through the remainder of the day. Outside, it was nighttime. The only light that came into the room emanated from the torches just outside the window. She could just barely make out where everything was in the small chamber.

She tried to get up to sit on the cot. Her luck was better this time, though she was still very weak. Skylet heard the muted voices of people moving past just outside the window, and she wondered what was happening and *where* those things were happening.

As she pondered those questions, Skylet reached over to the table and grabbed some of the fruit, consuming it slowly. Though she was famished, she feared that if she ate too quickly, she would vomit. Skylet took her time eating the juicy produce, and after a while, she began to feel the energy come back to her body. Her arms and legs began to feel stronger, the headache she experienced became lighter, and her senses returned.

Just as she was beginning to feel comfortable, there was a knock at the door. Skylet jumped and dropped a piece of sliced strawberry on the floor. "C-come in," she said, her voice still not back to normal.

The door opened and a man walked in holding a large lantern with several candles in a circular formation inside, which brought the room a considerable amount of light. Skylet recognized the man's face: Oros. With a yelp, she leapt off of the cot instinctually and ran to the very corner of the room. "You stay away from me," she said firmly, her voice coming back.

"Be calm," Oros responded. "I have no intention of hurting you."

"Where am I?"

"In a town called Selnes," he said. "My name is Oros, and I just want to speak with you."

Suddenly, Skylet became more aware of herself and realized something was missing: the cloak from Jessie and Séya. Her shoulders tensed as she hugged herself. "Where is my cloak?" she asked. "I'm cold." It was the best excuse she could think of as to why she might need it.

"Yes, the cloak," Oros said. "The one your mother gave you. It is safe."

"I want it back now. Give it to me, please."

"First, you answer my questions. Honestly. Then we can discuss the return of your cloak."

"Give me my cloak!" Skylet shouted as firmly as she could.

"Quiet, or you'll be locked in here forever!" Oros shouted back.

The two of them looked at each other in the silence of the room.

Oros took a breath and composed himself. "Please," he began. "I need your help."

"For what?" Skylet spat back.

Oros stepped more into the room and took a seat in a

chair nearest the door. He looked at her intently and spoke. "Where is the dragon hiding?"

"I told you before. I haven't seen a dragon."

"No?" Oros asked calmly. "And how do you think I found you?"

Skylet didn't answer. She hadn't the slightest idea.

"I've faced many dragons in my time. The smell of dragon fire is unmistakable. I smelled it on your cloak when we crossed paths in the forest and traced the scent all the way to you." He paused. "I know you've seen a dragon."

Skylet was noticeably flustered; her breath began to quicken.

"Where is it?" he asked.

"Why? So you can kill her like you killed my brother?" Skylet asked, tears forming in her eyes.

"I killed no one's brother."

"Your cloak is made from his skin, is it not?"

Oros didn't respond. He looked at his cloak and back at Skylet.

"Answer me!" she demanded.

"I fought a dragon some time ago, but he was severely injured when we met, the work of other soldiers. Not mine." He paused and looked down at the floor. "He was going to die anyway."

Skylet broke down and began sobbing uncontrollably. Oros stood up and walked toward her.

"Stay away from me!" exclaimed Skylet through tears. "I'll hurt you, I swear."

"My family was killed by a dragon," Oros said. "This very town, destroyed by a beast." He looked away from her and out of the window that was above the cot. "In the nearly twenty years since the destruction, Selnes has rebuilt itself. Still, though, the residue of the attack is felt here. If you know where to look, you can still find the charred remains of those who tried to escape unsuccessfully."

Skylet said nothing. All she could think at that moment was the last time she saw Arca. She wished more than anything that she could go back to that night and get to him before he left the cave. She would crawl to him with her broken leg, tell him how much she loved him, and beg him not to leave. But he was gone forever now, and she would never see him again. When she looked at the cloak upon Oros, the remnants of Arca draped over his shoulders, it made everything inside her burn to the core.

Oros turned his head back toward the girl and pulled out his necklace, at the end of which hung the large black claw. "This talon," Oros began, "came from the dragon that killed my uncle."

Skylet's eyes widened, Oros noticed.

"He handed it to me as he died, and I vowed to kill the dragon responsible. I will honor my uncle if it means the end of me."

"How do you know a dragon was responsible?" Skylet asked, sniffling. She searched for anything she could think of to call what he knew into question.

"Because I remember the battle," Oros responded. "And I saw this." He pulled out a large dark violet dragon scale from a pouch he had around his waist. "The very same color and type I saw near my uncle's body."

"I'll never tell you anything," Skylet said in a voice that sounded both defeated and firm, prepared for a battle. There was no other question she could ask, nothing else to say that would sway him.

"No matter," Oros said dismissively. "I will go back to Mysteya and track your witch friend the way I tracked you. I'm sure she will be more helpful."

Skylet gasped. "Wait! Please!"

Oros turned away from Skylet and picked up his lantern. Without looking back, he swiftly exited the room, slamming the door behind him, and leaving her alone in the darkness.

17.

Oros walked along the hallway with purpose. A rumbling in his stomach suddenly hit, giving him pause. He shook his head. Being so preoccupied with the notion of Skylet giving him answers about the dragon, Oros hadn't eaten.

He stopped inside a small empty kitchen, grabbing an apple from a bowl that sat in the middle of a wooden table. Adding cheese he had cut from some of the wrapped blocks nearby, he continued on his way.

He walked until he reached the end of the wide hallway, where there was a long brick spiral staircase that led upward. Oros went up the stairs and was greeted by another long hallway at the top. Soon, he came to a large door made of birch wood and entered the room.

Once inside, he took a small firesteel and a piece of rare black flint from the pouch that hung from his hip and lit the wall torches. It wasn't completely dark in the room to begin with, but it helped him to have more light while he attempted to enjoy his food in peace.

Of course, there were many other rooms for that purpose. Oros was, after all, at the old encampment for soldiers in Selnes. The place was mostly restored following the dragon attack years before, and was now used to store weapons of war. A handful of former soldiers only came in occasionally to maintain the building.

Oros sat in one of many rooms that contained dragon paraphernalia. From heads and limbs of the creatures to various armors coated with the skin of dragons. Swords and other weapons made of the sparkly Moonbeam Metal lined the walls, mounted like revered trophies. Any hunter would thoroughly enjoy perusing the room's contents. Skylet, however, would undoubtedly be mortified in such a place.

Oros had spent so much of his life studying dragons that he felt most at home there as he pondered what he might do next about his uncle's killer.

He took a bite of the apple, pairing it with a piece of the aged cheddar cheese, and remembered his uncle, who had first introduced him to the two flavors. As unpleasant and off-putting as the pairing was to young Oros, he grew to appreciate the taste of such a simple treat as he got older. Ruminating on what a connoisseur of food his uncle was, Oros admired how even the most elementary dish created far beyond the walls of great palaces, the most earthy and humble of meals, the man could fall in love with.

It seemed funny to Oros that Uncle Servalan, one of the greatest Dragonhunters around, would wax poetic about the many flavors they came across on their travels as much as he would about the skill it took to battle dragons. While he was a hunter, it was not something he took great pleasure in. He held dragons in the highest regard.

Refusing to use Dragon's Blood to heal any scars he received in battle, Servalan saw them as reminders to respect the majestic creatures. For him, hunting dragons was about duty and the responsibility to protect, which is what he tried to impart to his nephew.

Oros ate while staring intently at a scaled robe hanging from a hook near some of the weapons. It was Skylet's cloak. He sat his plate on a barrel near him and stood up to walk over to it, pulling it off the hook.

He held it, gently examining the scales of the dark violet garment. Oros marveled at the feel of it, which in many ways, was both like any other dragon he ever came across, yet different. It had greater thickness, but it felt as flexible as a bedsheet.

Oros stroked it and walked back to the chair, cloak in hand. "Where are you?" he asked as if he were having a conversation with the mantle and draped it over his knees, touching it once.

Before he could lift his hand to touch it again, he felt a brief hot flash come over him. The cloak suddenly became warmer as he held it. It was as if the garment might burst into flames at any moment. A spot in the center of his chest also became warm and tingly.

Oros felt himself beginning to sweat and quickly stood from his chair, dropping the cloak on the floor. He found himself breathless as he looked down at the ruffled article and saw steam rising from it.

After a moment or two, the heat dissipated. Oros went into his shirt and pulled out the dragon claw, which was noticeably warmer than usual, his hand tingling as he held it. He looked at the talon and back at the cloak, beginning to realize a bond between the two items. His eyes narrowed, and his head tilted as he tried to figure out what it was about the cloak that made it react so. Could it even *react*, as if guided by some force?

Oros pondered that question, among others. Was it alive? Did it have a soul? There were whispers of such things he recalled hearing as a child, though he never cared about that. Yet, one story occurred to him as he stood over the cloak.

Beginning their study of the creatures they would one day swear to hunt as young men, Uncle Servalan and Oros's father learned of a scarf interwoven with dragon skin. It could change its shape, even strangle someone to death by some mysterious influence. Was this cloak similar? Oros hadn't thought of that tale in years. For it to reach the surface of his mind as he considered what lay before him seemed a curious twist of fate. Servalan was speaking to him.

He thought for a second more before kneeling to cautiously touch the robe. It still felt warm, but it was cooler than it had been before he dropped it. He gingerly picked it up, hung it back on the hook near the weapons, and then stepped away from it.

Oros wondered whether it was worth his time to go back and talk to Skylet when she wouldn't give him any answers. Then he thought of making good on his promise to go back to Mysteya and find Séya. The hunter didn't know just yet what he should do, but he was confident that the cloak was special. Turning away from it, Oros left the room, thinking about what his next move would be.

18.

Jessie sat with her head bowed, and her eyes closed in the grassy patch. She was restless as if she were in a bad dream. The dragon shook while her wings and tail twitched in ways that looked like muscle spasms. The surface of her scales glistened with sweat.

Jessie saw flashes of light in the darkness of her closed eyes. Muffled sounds came to her, but she couldn't make anything out clearly. Then she began to see shapes and colors of all kinds. Still, nothing was clear. The dragon sat for a long while, enduring the discomfort.

Séya awoke from her sleep upon hearing the deep grumbling sounds that came from Jessie. She rushed to the dragon and called to her. "Jess," Séya reached up to touch her friend and felt the dampness of her scales. "Oh, dear Jessie," she said. She couldn't understand what was happening.

The old woman ran to grab a wooden bucket and filled it with water, bringing it back to sit with Jessie, and gently began wiping the dragon's brow with the cool liquid.

Jessie continued to shake and twitch, which intensified until it suddenly stopped and she heard a voice as clear as if it were right next to her.

"Where are you?" the gruff voice said.

She saw a hand reach out and stroke her face, it seemed. Then she began to notice objects around the hand. Torches along the walls lit the room she saw into. She noticed the mounted dragon heads and limbs, along with weapons that had killed or maimed other dragons.

At the sight of these, she growled and grumbled heartily. Then she saw his face. Oros looked curiously into Jessie's eyes, studying her through the cloak. Then, Jessie fell from his lap and onto the floor.

Looking up at him, she saw him pull out a claw that hung from around his neck. Her missing talon hand tingled, and she grumbled again. Oros picked her up and walked her to the corner of the room before everything faded away, and Jessie's vision was no more.

She slowly opened her eyes and came back to herself to feel Séya gently moving a folded wet cloth across her brow. "Are you all right?" Séya asked. "What did you see, dear?"

"The face of Skylet's captor," Jessie said. "The hunter she spoke of."

Séya looked intently at the dragon. "Where is he?" she asked.

"Selnes."

There was silence between them. Jessie stood up and moved away from the grass area in the center of the cave. She stood under a nearby waterfall to cool off, taking a deep breath before turning to Séya, who was standing not far away. "Are you ready?" asked the dragon.

Séya nodded.

"We can make it there well before daybreak."

"We'll have to move quickly to retrieve her if we hope

to not be noticed by the townspeople. They haven't seen a dragon in almost twenty years. It'll be very dangerous."

"Yes," Jessie replied almost to herself. Her brow furrowed. She struggled with thoughts of what sort of pain Skylet might be in, what tortures she might be enduring.

The dragon let out a deep sigh and kneeled to allow Séya, who had just finished putting on her boots and scarf, onto her back. Jessie climbed the cave wall and moved into the hole where she slept. The dragon picked up the yellow-orange pin from Skylet's cloak and put it into a pouch, which she handed to Séya before climbing into another hole in the cavern that led to an opening.

The dragon stared up at the night sky, stars twinkling back at her. They seemed to be speaking words of weightlessness. Words of happiness and hope. Words that if Jessie were not so overcome with concern, might have made her smile and feel comforted. Instead, she felt almost teased and irritated by the happy twinkling conversation the stars seemed to be having. She wanted to be a part of the interaction. She wanted Skylet there to share it with.

The dragon knew that Séya usually felt at peace with the stars at night, but at that moment, she could feel her friend struggling to find that peace as she stared at the starry night sky to keep from worrying about Skylet. They both fought as best they could, imagining the worst.

Jessie was determined, driven, even if she was afraid for Skylet's life. She was ready to do anything she could to make sure it was not too late. Jessie stood, allowing the wind to breeze around her.

"Let's get our Skylet," Séya said.

With that, Jessie pushed off and flew swiftly into the night.

19.

Skylet sat on the cot with her knees against her chest. She worried about Jessie and Séya, wondering whether or not their lives were in danger as she allowed her body to slide from against the wall and onto the cot.

Just then, the door to the room opened forcefully, and Oros stepped in quickly, grabbing Skylet's arm and pulling her away before she could avoid him. "Stand up," he demanded.

Skylet slipped away from him and kicked him in the shin.

Oros grunted and grabbed her again. "Come with me!" he spat, pulling her by the arm out of the room. He resorted to dragging her along the hallway and up the long staircase that led to the armory where he had been earlier.

She fought and tried to escape to no avail. When they reached the room, he pushed her through the doorway. "Sit there," he said, pointing to the chair where he sat before.

Skylet did so, out of breath.

Oros moved to the corner of the room, grabbed the cloak, and threw it at her. It draped over her lap like a wet noodle. "What is this?" he asked her.

Skylet sniffled. "A cloak," she responded testily.

Oros slowly stepped toward her as he spoke. "I held the cloak," he said, "and it grew hot. It is a magic cloak?"

"No," Skylet said.

"Is the dragon magic?"

"I don't know."

"You're lying," he said.

"I'm not!"

"You *are!*"

"I'm *not!*"

"*Put it on!*"

Skylet sat defiantly, sending Oros a venom-filled stare.

He slowly unsheathed a knife from his belt and let the hand holding it drop carelessly to his side. The two stared daggers at each other.

"Put it on," Oros said calmly with an undercurrent of something in his voice that Skylet didn't like.

She waited a moment before slowly rising to very deliberately put on the cloak.

"Out," Oros said, pointing to the door behind her.

Skylet turned and exited the room. Oros followed, his knife still drawn.

***

Jessie and Séya flew low over the cool water of the ocean. They didn't speak to each other at all during the trip, carrying the heaviness that hung over them as they cut through the air.

Selnes was the closest neighboring town north of Mysteya across the water. It was known throughout many lands as the place that suffered the most devastating dragon attack in recent memory. Those who survived called it The Great Slaughter of Selnes. Yet, it was a place that warmly welcomed many from every walk of life, and once boasted beautiful attractions, the likes of which one might come across behind the walls of a royal palace.

The largest ever monarch butterfly sanctuary, which included few rare silver-winged butterflies, was a sight in Selnes that many traveled from great distances to see. For years, it was the town's crowning jewel, until the culinary institutions and eateries began to appear and gain prominence. At its peak, Selnes was one of four places where those interested in learning how to cook made their pilgrimage.

Renowned artists and scribes sang the praises of Selnes while marveling at how secure they felt there as compared to other places. Major crime was such a rare occurrence and usually came with outsiders, but when trouble was imminent, an elite force of men and women known as The Sentinels protected the city as they had done for nearly a century.

Following the dragon attack, the number of protectors had greatly diminished. In an effort to maintain order in the aftermath, a temporary partnership was formed with the local protectors and the military of Selnes until The Sentinels reached their former numbers.

Almost two decades later, that uneasy partnership was still in place, and Selnes was now barely recognizable, far removed from its former greatness. Despite that, it moved ever forward, hopeful to one day return to its perch as the town that all others strived to emulate, content to survive another day.

After some time of flying in the darkness, land was

near. Water could be heard in the distance crashing against the coast. As they got closer, Jessie felt a wave of heat in her chest as they prepared their approach. When they touched down on the shore, they took a second to survey their surroundings. "The outskirts of Selnes," Jessie said.

Séya remembered traveling to Selnes a few times in her youth to collect treats for the many children she knew back in Mysteya. She noticed the candy sweet ocean breeze scent she recalled encountering whenever landing there was no longer present. The air now smelled like that of a typical shore.

Jessie looked up at the sky, then out on the horizon. Day would break soon. They had to move.

"How can we reach Skylet from here?"

"I need a moment to search," replied Jessie. The dragon closed her eyes and sat in a meditative state, attempting to search for the girl. Suddenly she felt another wave of heat in her chest. This one was much stronger. She physically reacted and grunted at the sensation.

"What's wrong?" Séya asked, concerned.

Jessie didn't respond as she opened her eyes. She placed the palm of her hand flat on the rocks of the shore and felt a faint vibration. The dragon began taking ginger steps until she reached the sand of the beach. Jessie continued up a hill that led to a vast coastal redwood forest. Every few seconds, she would feel the sensation of the heat in her chest and rumbling from the ground.

"Jess," Séya said. "Where are we going?"

"Pain, Séya." Jessie replied. "I feel great pain pulling."

They moved through the thick of the forest and came to a steep slope that led down to a dark and wide ditch.

The sensations Jessie felt were more potent and more consistent. She groaned. Séya stroked her comfortingly as they stopped to look down the large ditch. "Why have we stopped?" Séya asked.

"We must move down there."

Séya looked up at the dragon, who was staring intently down the trench. She started to question it, but decided not to and began walking. Jessie followed. They tried to be as careful as they could so they wouldn't slip and tumble down. When they reached the bottom, they stood there. Jessie groaned again.

"What do you think?" Séya asked as she walked along the uneven surface of the ditch.

Jessie didn't respond. She seemed to be scanning the surface for some clue as to why they were there. Séya did likewise, continuing to walk along until she accidentally kicked something stubborn in the dirt. She knelt and saw a shiny rock among the soil. The sparkly alloy looked familiar to her.

"Moonbeam Metal," she said to Jessie. "Is this the pain you feel?" She looked at the dragon, who shook her head.

"No," she said.

Séya tried to pick up the rock, but it wouldn't budge. She stood up and attempted to kick it, but it maintained its position as the thick dirt around it was brushed about. That was when Séya realized it wasn't a rock, but the tip of something. She knelt again and began digging. The deeper she dug, the more metal revealed itself. "Help me, please, Jess," Séya said.

The dragon thrust her large hands in the dirt and dug with all her force, throwing about heaping piles of earth. The two of them dug and dug until it became clear that what they stood upon was the large lid to some sort of hatch made entirely of Moonbeam Metal. There didn't seem to be a way to open it, as there was no visible handle or lock.

The two looked at each other. They seemed to need a moment to take in their discovery.

"What do you suppose is in there?" Séya asked.

"Pain."

"How do we open it?"

The dragon tilted her head, wincing. "Stand behind me," Jessie said.

Séya hopped behind the dragon and leaned against her back. With a deep breath, Jessie stood tall and spread her wings as far as they could go. When she couldn't take in any more air, she exhaled, unleashing an unimaginable force of fire, which had a slight liquid quality.

She concentrated all of her focus on the hatch for what seemed like an eternity to Séya. The dirt and brush around them began to catch fire but stayed in the ditch. Séya put her hands out and did her best to contain the surrounding fire by taking away oxygen from the flames so as not to alarm anyone nearby.

When Jessie finished, she composed herself before deeming it safe for Séya to come from behind her.

The Moonbeam Metal was melting into the hole of the hatch. They waited until the lid was gone, noticing complete darkness in the pit save for a small red-orange light signifying the molten metal reaching the ground below.

Though the hole had expanded from the burning, Jessie was too large to fit into it. Séya rubbed Jessie's shoulder and opted to climb down herself, but was worried about there not being an easy way down. "If you provided some light, I could see how to get down there," Séya said.

"Stand aside," said Jessie. The dragon shot a large fire dart into the hole, which went all the way down to the ground. The bottom was farther than Séya wished; nevertheless, she was going inside.

"I would have preferred an easier way in," she said.

"It doesn't look as if this was designed for anyone to go in or out, Séya."

"No, I supposed it doesn't. At least not from here."

Jessie winced. "Something is here," she said. "Find it, Séya. Make this pain stop."

The old woman nodded. "I will try, my friend." Séya turned away, and without a second thought, she jumped into the hole. The wind zipped against her face, making it difficult to keep her eyes open. If she were to manage not spraining or breaking a limb, she would have to time her landing just right.

A split-second later, Séya quickly waved her right hand toward the floor of the hole, and a powerful burst of air shot up to break her fall, allowing her to gracefully land on her feet, wobbling a bit. She stayed herself to catch her breath, kneeling to regain her composure. That display of her abilities required more energy than she was willing to let on.

"All right!" she shouted up to Jessie. Séya looked ahead and began slowly walking through the space. She couldn't see anything, as there was no light ahead of her, but she persisted. She kept to her right, hugging a rough brick wall.

The old woman felt her way along until she reached a dead end. She put her hand out to touch what was in front of her and felt a thick wooden surface. It felt to her, very worn and warped as if it had been sitting in the cold and dank darkness for a long time. Séya's palms searched for where a doorknob would be but found none. Trying to push the door in, she realized it wouldn't budge. Then Séya gave the door one hearty pound, and the sound reverberated along the walls throughout the hallway. Then, silence.

Séya took a breath and exhaled, placing both of her palms against the surface of the door and stepping in to lean her forehead against it. She closed her eyes and began muttering something under her breath, speaking softly to the door as if she were comforting a child. Séya's hands began to shake and the door shook with her.

She leaned in, straining only slightly before the door began to move backward. She was able to take one full step, and then the door fell inward, loudly crashing to the floor like the large tree from which the door was fashioned. The sound of the impact echoed throughout the darkness.

Before silence could return to the new space where Séya found herself, she heard a grumble, some sound that came from deep within the room. Though her eyes had begun to adjust to the darkness, she moved cautiously. An injury was the last thing she wanted. Séya took a breath and continued to move in carefully. After two steps, she knelt. Then she went lower until she was lying on her belly, beginning to crawl.

She moved straight ahead at a consistent pace, crawling until she noticed that the floor trailed off and went into a downward slope. She couldn't tell how far down it went or how steep it was just yet, but she continued to crawl until she began to lose control and started slipping. Before she ended up in a full slide, she managed to turn her body around so she was moving feet first. Down she went quickly until she fell onto a bed of small rocks.

As she tried to gain her bearings, Séya heard a sound that unnerved her: something was breathing. Whatever it was, it felt close to her and drew deep, calm breaths.

Séya slowly stood up and stepped gingerly on the rocks, leaning against the wall where the slide ended. Moving along, she realized that she was in a dungeon of some kind. A faint fruity smell tapped Séya's nose, and another grumble came from the darkness. It sounded pained and exhausted. Judging by what she heard, whatever was down there with her felt large.

"Hello," Séya spoke into the darkness. She heard slow shuffling on the rocky floor with her and moved quickly to her right as if to avoid an attack, but there was none. Only heavy and deep rhythmic breathing.

Séya got back down on her knees and began crawling on straight ahead. She felt in front of her in order to get a sense of what might be at arm's length, grasping more and more rocks until she touched a surface that made her pull her hand away and gasp. It felt dry and very rough, like the skin of a houndfish. The old woman reached out once more and gently touched the scaly surface. She quickly realized that it felt very familiar.

Crawling closer, she felt something else like tubes coming from the creature. Suddenly, the ground began to shake.

Séya yelped and moved away in an attempt to climb up the wall and get out of the pit, but it was no use. She couldn't think fast enough to use a spell to get herself out, but hoped something would come to her. Séya began muttering words and before she could finish, she noticed a dim light surrounding her. The shaking stopped.

Certain that neither the illumination nor the sudden stillness was at all her doing, Séya found herself confused. A gust of wind pushed her against the wall.

Slowly, she turned around to see that the entire pit, rocks and all, was lit beneath her. Séya stood in shock, realizing she was now staring at the face of a large, beaten, and broken-looking dragon.

20.

Séya's eyes widened. She was in awe as she looked over the bluish-black dragon that was breathing more calmly. She suddenly became aware of vibrations, a consistent thumping coming from the ground, which she assumed was the emaciated creature's heartbeat. Tears formed in her eyes as she noticed large tubes protruding out of each side, which led to the very ceiling of the dungeon.

The weathered dragon grumbled, looking at the old woman with tired eyes. Séya saw puncture wounds and many scars, some enormous and deep, others smaller. All about the prisoner's massive body and face, the marks of pain were laid bare. What was most troubling to Séya, though, was that the wings were missing. She noticed scars of what looked to her like long lightning rods where the wings should be. "Oh," Séya began. "You poor dear." She touched the dragon's nose and stroked it upward. Reaching out widely, Séya placed her hands on the creature's cheeks as if she could hold its face. "Who has done this to you?"

The prisoner breathed deeply and exhaled with a painful groan.

Séya began to cry. She didn't know what to do to help,

except stroke the dragon's face before stepping in closer to embrace its massive head. Looking at the lit ground, she noticed a small bunch of berries and other fruits lying inches away, which further upset her. Much of it had started to rot. "This is not enough for you to eat," she said under her breath.

Just then, there was a muffled rumble that came from the ceiling above. Séya jumped back from the dragon and looked up as another crash hit.

BOOM!

Dust and pebbles began to fall. It felt like an earthquake. Everything shook, and the ceiling was starting to cave in.

The dragon didn't bother moving. It let out an exhausted groan and gingerly lowered itself to the floor, covering its head with its hands as a child might do. The shaking of the pit area became more violent with each rumbling thud.

Séya quickly climbed on to the back of the large captive, avoiding the tubes and brushing the dust off of its rough surface. She laid down, so she was back to back with the dragon and did her best to avoid dust and rocks so that the debris didn't get in her face. The old woman stretched out her hands, palms facing the ceiling and closed her eyes, bracing herself.

Half of the ceiling crashed in, nearly covering the area where Séya and the dragon were. Large fragments would have injured them, but the sorceress produced a magical shield in the shape of a dome made of air and a sky-blue-tinted light that protected them. Séya held her position until she was sure nothing else would fall on to them. With one push of the shield to her left, all the rocks and dirt fell aside as the shield disappeared.

Séya looked up at the gaping hole in the ceiling and noticed that daylight was coming. It looked to her that there was a building made of brick above the dark dungeon where the imprisoned dragon had been kept. Jessie had destroyed much of it breaking through to the dungeon.

As the sorceress climbed up from the slope of rubble, she could see her friend's hunched silhouette standing over a nearby mound of wreckage, looking like an avenger of some sort who came to the rescue. The two locked eyes, and Séya slowly reached her hand up to signify that she was okay.

21.

Jessie slowly moved toward the pit until she reached her friend. She put her hand out, and Séya extended herself to touch it. They were palm to palm for a moment. Jessie's was shaking and felt unusually warm to Séya. "Come," she said, taking Jessie's large hands within her much smaller ones. She led the dragon to the head of the trench.

Jessie groaned audibly. "So much pain here, Séya. . ."

"I know." Séya released Jessie and crawled back down the cavity to face the weakened prisoner that only looked up to recognize Séya, its eyes half-closed.

Jessie looked into the face of the broken and gaunt dragon, which was as large as she, her heart was in pain to witness such a pitiful sight. Straddling the edges of the pit, Jessie tried to get a better look at the captive. She leaned her head in closer, and Séya moved out of the way.

The weakened creature slowly lifted its head, which seemed a strenuous act. Sensing this, Jessie used her hands to gently hold its head up. "Tell me, sister," Jessie said, her tone nurturing, "how came you to be here?" Their foreheads touched, their eyes closed and Jessie saw it. The pain in its entirety and eternity was as terrible as the worst pain she had ever known; Jessie felt it all.

The dragon's name was Ulonae. She once could speak and even sing. Possessed with a most beautiful voice, she was excited to share it with her children. Jessie could hear the melodious sounds as if they came from within her. Ulonae returned home from searching for food for her babies who would be hatching soon. Two of her eggs had been cracked, the unborn dragons lying still as though they were asleep. One egg was missing, which she found not far from the cave. None of her children survived the night.

The moment she realized that her babies were gone forever, her ability to speak was lost. There was no one to share her stories with now. No one to pass her lessons down to. Her response was a visceral one.

She rampaged through the town of Selnes and burned it to the ground, killing many people in the process. After much fighting with the local soldiers and much destruction, Ulonae was captured. They cut off her wings with blades of Moonbeam Metal and condemned her to the pit. She was kept alive just enough so that her heart could keep beating, providing the coveted Dragon's Blood for the wealthy and the army of Selnes over the years.

For many moons, Ulonae wanted to die. With her will to live properly shattered, she wanted to spite the world that took away her children, sentenced her to a prison, and kept her alive for her blood and nothing else. After many sleepless nights, she thought she would fall asleep one day for the last time and never wake up again.

Jessie felt all the memories and emotions that seemed to pour out of Ulonae. Their hearts and spirits were connected as everything began to make sense. In that instant, the two dragons were one and the same.

Jessie opened her tear-filled eyes and stared into Ulonae's, tears of her own streaming down her face like a quiet river. Jessie heard a voice speak to her that sounded like a kind of smoothness she had never known in all her years of living. "Thank you," the voice said. "Thank you for setting me free, Jessie."

"My sister Ulonae," Jessie said through tears. "Your suffering is done."

The two dragons held each other, Ulonae suddenly gained enough strength to lift her arms and touch Jessie's hands with her own. A shift happened within, and Jessie could sense it. They embraced tightly; the entire pit lit up around them brightly. They cried together as Séya stood by and watched.

Then, Ulonae's strength abandoned her. Her body became still in Jessie's arms as if she were being rocked to sleep. The bright light around them faded, and the former prisoner's breathing stopped. All was silent.

Jessie continued to hold Ulonae in her arms, taking a deep breath before releasing her, gently laying her head down against the ground. "Be at peace dear sister," she said. "May you be comforted by the spirits of your children."

22.

Skylet and Oros reached the top of a large tower in the building and entered a room. Minimally furnished, there were only a few chairs and a small table in the large diamond-shaped space. The floors and walls in the room were constructed of a smooth brick. Every step Skylet took felt as if she were walking along a surface as soft as grass. The room felt less like it belonged in an encampment than it did a castle to her.

"Keep moving," Oros said from behind her. "Toward the window."

They walked toward a tall floor-to-ceiling window that Skylet realized was a set of luxurious glass double doors with golden flower and tree designs bordering the edges.

"Open it," Oros instructed.

Skylet slowly pushed the large glass doors open and saw a long smooth brick walkway before her. Flowers in small pots flanked the barriers on each side of her, slowly becoming more visible as the sky brightened with the rising sun as day more rapidly approached.

"Go," said Oros.

"Where?" Skylet snapped.

"You only have one option."

She moved forward, and Oros closely followed. They continued all the way to the edge of the walkway and stood near the high railing. A gentle breeze moved between and around them like smooth drapes.

"What are we doing here?" Skylet asked.

"I used to come here from time to time and watch the sun rise and set," Oros said. "Overseeing the land, I was able to gain a different appreciation of the destruction this place has suffered."

Selnes had come a long way in the almost two decades since the dragon rampage. But, there were still parts near the outskirts that had been mostly untouched. As the sun rose higher, large sections of damaged land and destroyed old brick buildings were more visible. Remnants of the forests nearby that burned to the ground were just beginning their return. Selnes was still healing.

"I look out over this town, and I wonder what my parents' last thoughts were as they were burned alive." Oros stood next to Skylet as they both looked beyond the edge. "I wonder if my young sister was at least wrapped in the arms of my mother at the time."

Silence. Oros continued. "There was nothing to save my family from a blood thirsty dragon."

Skylet looked over at Oros before stepping away toward the flowers nearest her.

"If your cloak is magical, as I believe it is," reasoned Oros, "maybe it'll do its work and save you."

"Save me?" Skylet asked.

Before she understood what was happening, Oros picked her up over his shoulder and threw Skylet over the railing.

23.

Skylet was locked in a free fall. The girl screamed, her arms and legs flailing. She was in disbelief. The exchange took place too quickly for her to have any warning.

Oros watched intently, waiting for something miraculous to happen. Skylet's cloak flapped, and he let out a quiet gasp. For a second, it looked as if it would make her glide to the ground gracefully. But instead, she fell faster.

Just then, a loud whoosh came from above. Oros turned around quickly and looked up to find an even bigger surprise than he could have bargained for: Jessie and Séya swooped in toward him like a hawk closing in on its kill. The dragon dove straight for Oros with venom in her eyes. Séya let out a battle cry as Jessie's large head crashed into Oros, knocking him through the barrier of the walkway and down toward the ground below.

Before they flew too low, Séya swiftly jumped off of Jessie's back and landed on what was left of the walkway edge. She watched as Skylet fell farther to her impending doom and quickly made sweeping gestures with her arms and hands. The sorceress strained and stomped her foot, leaning firmly in as she put her hands in a grappling position.

Skylet's fall was stopped with only feet to go before she hit the ground. Séya's arms were shaking, as if she were carrying a great weight. She held her position, Skylet's body floating in midair. Then, she gently lowered the girl to safety.

At the same time, Jessie and Oros crashed into a nearby birch tree, knocking it over as they tumbled to the ground only feet away from where Skylet now stood. The fall of Jessie's large body resulted in a trembling of the earth beneath her as she tried to collect herself. Nearby homes rumbled, and residents quickly scrambled outside, startled by the ruckus. They ran to the nearest neighbor's door to see after each other's wellbeing.

Oros staggered to his feet as he looked at the dragon he had been searching for all along. Jessie seemed to recover from the fall more quickly. The two stood across from each other, examining one another.

"Finally," Oros said to himself under his breath. "I've found you."

"Hunterrrr," Jessie said with a hint of a growl. She spoke no further words. Her body was low, like an animal of prey. She was ready to kill.

Oros slowly pulled out the talon that hung around his neck. "This must be yours," he said to Jessie.

The dragon felt a strong tingling sensation that burned in the area where her missing talon used to be. It was as if she had just lost it at that second. She let out an angry roar toward Oros, who was unfazed.

Rays from the sun peeked just above the mountains. The morning had come. It would not be the quiet start that many other mornings had been. For as expected, no one was pleasantly surprised to see a giant beast in town so close to their homes. There were too many unpleasant memories.

Oros stared into his talon necklace before moving his eyes away from it and deliberately toward Jessie. It was as though he were scanning her body to find the best place to strike a devastating blow. "If you would like it back," he began, gently rubbing the smooth surface of the talon between his index finger and thumb. "I challenge you to take it from me!" Oros released the talon and let it hang on his neck like a prized medallion. Then he pulled a sword from the sheath strapped over his shoulder and let the tip of it touch the ground.

Jessie moved rhythmically, pacing from left to right while staring at her opponent. She began to feel the spirit of Arca as she looked at the cloak Oros wore. The dragon thought back to his throwing Skylet over the balcony and her emotions boiled over. She gritted her teeth, smoke escaping in thin wisps from her flared nostrils as she snarled.

Oros drew a line in the dirt with his sword and stepped just behind it. He lowered his body as if he were readying himself to jump, staring into the yellow-orange eyes of the enemy, which trained on him. Oros took the talon, that hung around his neck and kissed it. "I'm here, Uncle," he said to himself.

Jessie roared again, and without any further notice, she charged at the Dragonhunter. As she ran like a wild animal, her body raised, she drew a deep breath. When she exhaled, a massive wave of fire swiftly came straight at Oros.

He seemed to be mesmerized by the beauty and power of the fire, watching as it came closer and closer. At the very last second, he roused himself, switched hands with his sword from his right to his left, and grabbed the right side of his cloak, bringing it over himself to block the wave of flames that engulfed him.

He stayed covered for only a second before moving the cape away from himself to strike at Jessie, who was charging at him through the flames.

Oros swung his sword heartily in an attempt to cut Jessie, but she seemed ready for such an attack.

She jumped into a somersault, flapping her wings once to fan the flames around him.

Landing behind him, she swiftly swiped her large tail along the ground to trip Oros up.

The hunter wasn't fast enough to avoid it, being knocked off balance. He recovered by sticking his sword into the ground and pushing off of it, somersaulting in the air.

Jessie tried to shoot him with a fireball, but Oros quickly used his cloak again to bat the ball of fire back toward the dragon, where it struck her in the chest, disappearing into a puff of smoke.

Oros had just enough time to claim his sword before Jessie tried to slash at him with the sharp talons of her hands, narrowly missing him as he spun around into the swipe. There was a beauty in how they moved amidst the intensity of the battle.

He came out of the spin and slashed Jessie's arm with his sword. The dragon howled in pain and jumped back as she tried to smash him into the ground with her tail, slamming it down with all her force, the earth rumbling in its wake.

Oros dodged it and raced toward the dragon.

Blood slowly began to trickle from Jessie's forearm. The intense tingling sensation she felt coupled with the pain was too familiar to her. There was no mistaking that Oros's blade was made of Moonbeam Metal.

The flames around them began to spread outward from where they were, slowly moving closer to the homes of residents who lived nearby. People quickly came out with wooden buckets of water and began trying frantically to put the fires out, or they simply took their children and few belongings and fled the area for the hills in case the fire destroyed their homes.

Skylet and Séya looked on, neither of them knowing what to do next. Séya turned away for a moment and noticed how close the fire was getting to nearby homes. "Come with me, girl," she said to Skylet as she rushed in to contain the fire. She couldn't think about what people might do when she used her magic to save them. She needed to act. "Help get those children to safety!"

Skylet ran toward a brother and sister she saw holding hands quickly chasing after their parents. The boy tripped over himself and fell to the dirt, taking his smaller sister with him. "Come, little ones," said Skylet, helping the boy and his sister up. "Go, quickly!"

"Thank you," the boy said, shaken, as he ran off.

Skylet kept an eye out for others and ran into the thick of nearby commotion to help families get clear of danger before going back to be near Séya.

The fight raged on as the sun rose. Jessie flapped her wings forcefully, sending gusts of wind at Oros, pushing him back. The dragon slowly moved toward him, continuing to push him closer to a nearby brick wall.

Oros's body rolled and skidded along the dirt until he

was against the wall and could go no farther.

In a brief second, her wings stopped flapping so she could get a good swipe at his face with her sharp talons. Claws scratched his cheek and moved down to his neck, narrowly missing his throat.

Oros fell to the ground face first.

Before Jessie could finish him off, he pulled out a small bag from behind his back and slammed it onto the ground, causing it to explode in a flash and a puff of white smoke that obscured the dragon's vision.

She expelled fire in an attempt to burn him, but he had moved from where he was.

Among the flame and smoke, Jessie turned around, making sweeping scratch motions trying to strike Oros. She roared in frustration at her failed attempts.

Suddenly, the dragon felt slashes on her leg and side. She let out a howl in pain as her arms and tail flailed every which way, hoping to connect with her enemy. Then she felt other strikes on different points of her body.

She dropped to the ground and felt yet more attacks; Oros moved swiftly like a predator of the shadows.

The dragon flapped her wings and took flight just above the fiery fog. As she hovered, she noticed the thick smoke dissipating and Oros running around like a buzzing fly that couldn't exit a tight space.

The dragon swooped back down toward him and the fight continued.

In the distance, Séya could hear rhythmic rumblings coming from a nearby forest. Faint at first, the old woman could hear them as she continued working to quell small fires. Skylet stood nearby and anxiously watched the battle. "Listen," Séya said. She had just successfully contained the closest fire to some of the homes.

"What is it?" Skylet asked. She stepped in and grabbed Séya's arm.

"It sounds like. . ." the old woman paused as the rhythmic marching grew louder. "Oh, no."

"What?" Skylet asked.

"Stay here," Séya said, leaving Skylet to watch the fight on her own.

The sorceress couldn't get too close to the battle because a large area was being overcome by a great deal of fire, more than she could contain. She got as close as she could before she attempted to make contact with her friend. "Jessie!" Séya cried.

The dragon didn't respond during her struggle. She continued to fight, which frightened Séya. She had never seen her friend behave so erratically. "We already have Skylet! We need to flee now!"

Skylet turned around, and then she understood. She felt a deep heat in her belly as the steps of fifty armored soldiers marched toward the battle site. In the far distance, she could see that they carried all sorts of weapons—from crossbows to swords—and she saw a very large bow on stone wheels that had to be pushed by four men.

Skylet jumped up and ran toward Séya, but she went a few steps farther, not feeling the heat of the fire that permeated the area. "JESSIE!" she screamed with all her force.

This seemed to get through to the dragon momentarily. She paused for a split second while in the middle of chasing Oros, whipping her tail about to stop him.

That was enough time for Oros to shift the momentum

of the battle in his favor. He slashed at Jessie's ankle with his sword, bringing her down to her knees and on her belly.

The hunter quickly climbed onto her back, holding the sword to her neck. Both of them were sweating, bleeding, and out of breath. "Do you remember this blade, dragon?" Oros whispered in Jessie's ear. "It once belonged to my uncle, a good man you killed."

Jessie turned her head upward slightly to catch Oros's eyes, and in a brief moment, she felt a hint of something that stirred confusing feelings within her.

"Now," Oros began. "Vengeance will be mine."

Before he could strike, she used every ounce of her strength to get herself up and give her wings one powerful flap, pushing off of the ground.

Oros tried to hang on, but he lost his grip and fell off of Jessie's back.

Before he hit the ground, she grabbed him with both her large hands, sharp talons digging into him, and slammed him on his back. He screamed in pain and then became stoic, as if accepting his defeat.

Jessie moved her large head in over his and stared him in the eyes. Oros could feel the heat of her breath against his face, expecting to be burned to a crisp in that instant. "Do it then," he said quietly.

She inhaled deeply, but instead of exhaling fire, she put her forehead against his and closed her eyes.

There was a flash of light, and then she saw a family inside a home. A man and woman stood over a crib, smiling and speaking in hushed tones. The dragon noticed a boy of 10-years old walking into the candlelit room toward a baby's crib. He stood over it and peered inside to see a small baby girl wrapped in a blanket.

Reaching in to the crib, he touched the girl's forehead gently and looked up at his mother and father; both parents lovingly rested a hand on the boy's head and shoulder, respectively. There was a warmth that filled the room, a comfort that Jessie felt so intensely.

Her sight drifted from the boy to the shadowy form of a tall man who appeared in the doorway across the room. The boy and his parents looked up from the baby in the crib, acknowledging the man's presence as he stepped into the space.

Jessie's vision of the figure in the memory was unfocused at first. But the longer she looked at the man, her perspective became clearer. The dragon shook inside, recognizing the silent and imposing individual to be the Dragonhunter she killed years ago. It was Oros's uncle, the great Servalan. She remembered the details of him as clearly as the memory she found herself inside of.

As she took in the sight, the dragon noticed the thin layer of sweat glistening just on the surface of his dark complexion. Extensive exposure to dragon fire had made him more tanned than he might already have been otherwise. Everything from the defined muscles of his arms to the lines and creases on his face seemed more prominent than she remembered. Jessie saw the visible scars upon his face and neck from the many battles he fought and recalled the respect she had for him as an opponent in spite of how challenging it was to see him in that instant.

She felt for a moment as though her past had come back to haunt her. But Jessie quickly pushed aside that thought, for she was not in Oros's memory to wallow in her past but to understand something about his.

Servalan stared at the boy, glancing once at the father who Jessie understood was a former Dragonhunter, having lost the lower part of his leg in battle. He touched his son's head with his hand, moving it to the boy's shoulder. The man gave his son two gentle pats before nudging him toward Servalan, who waited patiently for his new student.

Jessie next saw them leave Selnes on a boat together headed to an island where Oros would further his training as a hunter.

The memory jumped forward a month later. Word came to the island by pigeon messenger that Selnes had been all but destroyed by a dragon. Servalan and his nephew returned to find their home desolated, their family gone. There seemed to be no end to the depth of grief that lay heavily upon Oros and his uncle from what Jessie could feel.

Survivors were full of anger and wanted to destroy all dragonkind. They charged Oros's uncle, the last living member of the Dragonhunters of Selnes, to search nearby lands in order to wipe them out, preventing the beasts from coming back to their town.

Over the next few years Oros's training continued, and the two faced various dragons, Jessie included, and on more than one occasion. Through Oros's mind, she saw how he scaled the impossibly tall mountain in Quentanan to reach his uncle, who lay dying with her talon in his hand. The dragon was struck by the young boy's tenacity and was astonished his body didn't give out before he reached the top.

Jessie traversed through other memories and saw many other dragons Oros had faced over the next several years following his uncle's death. Dragon after dragon, she saw either fell by his hand or had been maimed and left for soldiers or others to claim for whatever purpose they had in mind.

For Jessie, witnessing the mutilation of so many dragons was like being stabbed many times over; she almost couldn't stay within Oros's memories it stung so badly. But then she saw one memory that pained her very soul. It was a memory involving Arca.

Battered and beaten, Oros found him near death at the top of a tall hill that overlooked a valley. Arca possessed enough strength for just one more fight.

Jessie looked at him. Studying his bearing, noticing his injuries she saw how the slight trembling of his body seemed to betray his display of stoicism. There was something else about the dragon she raised that she felt so strongly: he had found the other dragon children.

At first, Jessie was surprised that he had succeeded in doing what he said he would. Then, when she considered it again, she was less than astonished. Of course, he had found them. For a moment she was embarrassed, wondering how she could have doubted him.

Somehow, from within Oros's memory, Jessie was able to tap into Arca's recollection of finding his dragon siblings. It was a feat Jessie had never before performed, and she found herself bewildered, trying to understand what happened.

The dragon reasoned that the intense emotions she felt after seeing Arca for the first time in years had pushed her into a new realm of her power that hadn't previously been explored. She couldn't be sure, but that seemed to be the best guess. Arca's memory lasted a second, but she was able to see where they were being held in a prison chamber, and how their captors surrounded him as he prepared to fight.

The memory faded, and Jessie was taken back to Oros's memory. She had only a second to readjust before Arca charged at the hunter, initiating a battle.

Jessie watched every moment, felt every charged emotion that raged between the two. It was not unlike her battle against Servalan. The desperation, the animosity she knew all too well.

As she stayed in the memory watching the grand struggle, she came to know something else by way of Oros's mind. Most of the dragons he faced were fearful and uncertain opponents, which made it easy for him to make short work of them. Something about Arca was different and touched Oros to his core. This dragon fought with both aplomb and abandon.

Arca was not only fearless, but he was also a formidable fighter. Jessie looked on, struck by how honorably they engaged with each other. She could see an articulate conversation of sorts taking place far beyond words, though it wasn't apparent to them just yet. The way the two moved reminded her a lot of how she and Skylet played Dodgefire.

In the midst of the fighting, Oros came to recognize that he was battling not with a heartless creature, but with a soul that felt much more familiar than he expected; one that harbored the same anger he carried within himself. In realizing this, Oros began to feel a deep kinship with Arca.

After a long while of fighting, it became clear that Arca was spent. So too was Oros, who no longer saw the battle as a challenge. He took pity on the dragon, something he hardly ever felt, especially when engaged in conflict. The two of them collapsed on the ground, out of breath and bruised. The opponents looked at each other, mere feet apart, managing to muster up enough energy to reach out and grab each other's hands in the way that brothers in arms might.

Jessie felt the connection; it was as if she herself made contact with Arca one last time. She felt his guilt and frustration over not freeing his siblings. Jessie wished desperately to comfort him and express how proud she was to witness his bravery and to feel the depths of his love for his family.

Oros and Arca held firm, never releasing each other, nor did they ever take their eyes off one another. When Arca finally stopped breathing, his eyes were still looking at Oros. The passion and fire he possessed still present, even in death.

The next thing Jessie saw was the young hunter finishing the process of burying the dragon's body. After standing at the makeshift grave in silence, Oros put on the cloak made of Arca's skin and began his journey to find her.

The memory jumped again to a more recent time. The dragon saw the moment Skylet and Oros crossed paths in the forest, and a connection made itself known to her.

"Your sister lives," Jessie's voice echoed in Oros's head. The dragon lifted her head, returning from the memories and back to the present time. She looked into Oros's widened brown eyes as the fire that surrounded them burned fiercely. Jessie looked to her right to see Séya and Skylet standing just beyond the flames. They were yelling something, but Jessie couldn't make out the words. "There," she said.

Oros slowly looked over in the direction Jessie had turned and saw his baby sister standing next to Séya.

24.

Jessie released Oros from her grasp and slowly backed away, allowing him space to stand and cautiously approach her. "Can it truly be?" he said in disbelief, his voice shaken.

"It is."

Oros fell to his knees and looked up at the dragon. "I don't know. . ."

"You don't have to," she said. "You are absolved from guilt and angst." She touched the top of his head with her large hand that was missing the talon. "You have carried so much anger with you for so long," Jessie expressed. "Release it now. Let it wash away."

Oros began to tremble. As Jessie removed her hand, an arrow suddenly struck her shoulder. Howling in pain, she staggered backward. The soldiers had arrived, shouting and ready for battle.

Séya and Skylet reacted. They tried to get the soldiers to stop, but there was so much commotion their voices could scarcely be heard.

Jessie pulled the arrow out, but another struck her near her neck. She fell over roaring and pulled that one out before quickly pushing off the ground and swooping into the army of soldiers. The dragon knocked away nearly the entire first line of defense with a whip of her wing. Then she turned and proceeded to breathe fire at the army as arrows flew her way. Men ran about ablaze. They screamed and rolled on the ground in an effort to put the flames out.

Some soldiers wore dragon skin with their armor; they were bolder. They were able to get under Jessie and viciously stab and cut her arms, legs, stomach, and tail. Some of them she was able to crush with her weight as she stepped around, but others darted out of the way to avoid further attacks. Still, she fought hard as the arrows and blades swarmed her like angry bees.

Then came the third wave of soldiers.

Séya jumped into the thick of the fighting, using sorcery to defeat the men. She threw them left and right with her hands from a distance, though she could feel her energy beginning to fade. Age suddenly a reminder that she could no longer sustain strenuous magic for long stretches of time as she could in her youth.

Saving Skylet from her drop earlier had also taken a toll, given her emotional state during the use of heavier magic. The deeper the well of feelings like love or anger when that kind of power is exerted, the more stamina is lost. Séya would need to rest very soon.

When arrows and other projectiles came her way, she conjured an invisible shield to stop them.

Meanwhile, Oros called to the soldiers. "Wait," he shouted. "Stop!" He ran into the battle with his sword drawn and attempted to subdue surviving soldiers who dared continue to strike down an angry dragon. He fought his way to the third wave and took some of them down before trying to get the attention of the soldier's general. "Please," he implored. "Cease your fighting! This dragon is peaceful!"

Oros subdued a few more soldiers before he was knocked over onto the ground from behind. Before he could get to his feet, a group of men picked him up and threw him into a nearby wall of fire. He screamed in pain, for the dragon skin he wore couldn't protect all of him.

"Witch!" one of the soldiers yelled across to Séya as she approached. "You'll be burned on this day."

Séya drew the nearby fire into her vicinity, gracefully using the full motion and range her body would allow. She set her feet and waved her arms as if confidently laying down colors on a canvas like a painter, able to manipulate the flames around her. They were transformed into a cascade of fire-rain that stung and nipped at most of the soldiers of the third wave as they scattered and dodged. It required her whole self to complete the spell, which depleted even more of her energy. She lost her balance and dropped to her hands and knees to catch her breath.

The large bow on wheels was set and ready to fire. The men positioned themselves at each of the points of the bow and used their weight to keep it steady as the soldiers took aim at Jessie, who continued to fight.

Skylet saw this and ran up to warn the dragon. "Jessie!" she called out.

The dragon saw from the corner of her eye, Skylet running to meet her. She jumped over a large group of soldiers to reach the young lady. "Skylet, you need to go!"

The girl kept running to Jessie, disregarding what she said.

Arrows, daggers, and spears cut through the air. Jessie

was hit by two of them, but she continued to run, batting away soldiers in the process. She had to make sure Skylet was safe. "Send this fireball toward them like we do for Dodgefire!" the dragon shouted.

Skylet nodded in understanding. They moved quickly.

Jessie shot out a short burst of fire and without missing a beat, Skylet took her cloak and swapped it in the direction of the soldiers. The ball exploded on the ground knocking them about. Skylet twisted into Jessie's arms, which enveloped her. "Dear child," the dragon said.

"We have to leave *now*, Jessie!" Skylet said quickly. She held the dragon as tightly as she could.

"Ready?" called one of the soldiers who stood at the large bow.

"Ready!" the soldiers responded.

"Fire!"

Another soldier behind the bow pulled a thick wooden lever, which sent a massive arrow tearing through the sky like a bolt of lightning.

Séya, still on her knees, saw this and, through force of will, pushed past her limit to use the last ounce of her energy to stop it. She spoke an incantation, and the large, thick piece of wood attached to the arrow began to dissolve into white sand. It started at the back end and quickly moved toward the top. By the time the metal arrow had begun to disintegrate, it had pierced straight through Jessie's wing, knocking over both her and Skylet.

"No! Jess!" Séya exclaimed as she tried running through the wave of soldiers to get to her.

"Grab the witch!" one of the soldiers yelled.

Séya fought them off as best she could, but she was hit over the back of her head with the hilt of a sword and quickly scooped up by two soldiers.

"To the dragon!" another soldier called. "It has fallen!"

Skylet was covered in Jessie's blood. "Jessie," she cried, breathing quickly.

"You must go now," the dragon said. "They are coming to take me."

Skylet was silent. She just kept caressing the dragon, even though the men were approaching. They wanted her precious blood. Both Jessie and Skylet knew that, but neither would say it aloud.

"Please, girl, you mustn't be captured. We came to free you."

"And you did," Skylet touched Jessie's face.

The dragon smiled and looked up at Skylet.

"I'm going to get you back."

"Leave!" the dragon growled.

Skylet jumped back, frightened. The two stared at each other as Skylet stepped away before breaking out into a run straight for the woods, leading to the rolling hills of the mainland.

"After her!" a commanding soldier ordered. Several of the others gave chase.

In the ensuing commotion, the men moved to collect the dragon. Oros managed to crawl just beyond the wall of flames where he covered himself in his cloak for further protection against burns.

He watched the soldiers all band together, lifting the dragon, who was in too much pain to fight back. She was put on a large cream-colored tarpaulin. The remaining soldiers heaved her up and carried the dragon away, while another carried an unconscious Séya over his shoulder.

Off they marched, victorious. After all, they had defeated a formidable dragon and captured a witch. They cheered and hollered and taunted Jessie, while Oros removed the hood from his cloak and watched them continue their march into the distance.

25.

Skylet ran as fast as she could through the woods, curving around thick oak trees and bursting through the bushes in an attempt to throw the soldiers off her trail. Yet, they persisted, and one of them even kept a good pace with her. She felt as though her lungs were on fire, and her legs began to tire out, but she continued to push herself.

Her eyes darted every which way, searching for an exit when she saw a large fallen tree ahead of her in the distance. She was sure she could clear it and keep going, reasoning that the weight of their armor and weapons would make it difficult for the soldiers to continue keeping up with her. She came closer and without giving it another thought, she jumped onto the log, but a crooked branch snagged the end of her cloak. She pulled it free, but she wasn't fast enough to clear the tree before the quickest soldier grabbed her and dragged her to the ground.

***

Oros slowly moved farther away from the flames behind him, which were beginning to die out. Bloody and burned, he crawled until he felt strong enough to stand up, but not before he noticed something in the dirt: a vial with a metal band around it, full of a plum-colored liquid. Dragon's Blood. Rather than use it, he picked it up and put it in a pouch hanging from the belt around his waist as he began walking in the direction Skylet had run.

He moved unhurriedly but kept a consistent pace. The pain from his wounds attacked him with each step. Smoke rising from his body and his clothes, he walked along, his breathing labored.

Each step he took felt heavier than the last, but he endured. He did his best not to groan or wince, continuing in the direction of some of the footprints he saw moving away from where all the fighting took place. Though parts of his face were burned and scraped, he could still smell. It was this sense that guided him in the direction Skylet had run.

Oros found himself moving on instinct, almost unaware that his body was in motion. The pain was so intense that he soon became numb to it. The hunter followed the tracks until they stopped, ruined by what looked to him to be a scuffle between the group. He had to rely on his nose from then on, following the smell of dragon fire that was essentially the same one he found on himself, but it was slightly different coming from Skylet. He followed a narrow dirt pathway deep into the woods until he heard the sudden and terrifying screams of a girl.

His paced quickened, shuffling his way near a large pine tree where he found a group of men holding Skylet's arms while one swiped at her with a large knife. "Are there any other dragons coming to attack us?" one soldier asked forcefully. When Skylet didn't answer, he slit her thigh.

She howled.

"Are there?!"

Oros watched, hidden nearby. When he saw another soldier pull out his sword and move closer, making ready to harm her, he noticed the cloak slowly moving in the background, stretching and flapping as it did when he threw her over the balcony before. The soldiers were unaware.

Skylet stared at the man with the sword, a look that was both fearful and angry on her face.

As Oros watched, he pulled out another one of the small bags from his waist pouch. With a well-timed step from behind a tree, he threw it at the group where it exploded into a large puff of white smoke upon hitting the ground. The window of opportunity was open for him to take his chance and move in with his sword drawn. Oros noticed the soldier in front of Skylet becoming quickly wrapped in what he thought to be the girl's cloak, though he didn't stop to consider how that was possible.

In seconds Oros was in the thick of the group. He moved almost as if he were completely free of injury, careful not to show any sign of weakness as he subdued at least two of the men. He managed a labored foot sweep, which tripped one up, while he knocked another in the forehead with the hilt of his sword.

In the same instant, he heard muffled screams from some of the others and frantic footsteps that sounded like they were moving away from the activity. After taking down another soldier, Oros knelt to the ground in the midst of the thick fog, covering himself with his hood. He waited, and when the smoke slowly cleared away, he looked up to find several soldiers disarmed and sprawled out on the ground, unconscious. Some were bleeding from various parts of their bodies and looked as if they had been sliced by blades.

Skylet was out of breath, leaning against the tree behind her. Oros saw that she was bleeding from her injuries as she looked out over the group of still bodies that lay in front of her. Her eyes met Oros's and stayed there for a moment before she released a heavy breath and slid off of the tree, passing out on the ground.

26.

Oros slowly stood up and removed his hood. He began walking toward Skylet, stepping over the battered and bloodied bodies of the men. When he reached her, he took a little while to examine her. She seemed peaceful to him somehow.

He was suddenly overcome with emotion, looking at the young woman before him; a woman who was once a child he thought long dead. Wiping away tears, he winced. The salt from them irritated the burns on his face.

Oros took a breath and knelt next to her, assessing the damage to her body. He took note of the wounds she sustained. Scanning her, his eyes made their way to the cloak that wrapped over her leg. He carefully reached out to touch it, anticipation building within him that something would happen. Maybe the mantle would attack him. Maybe it would wrap itself around Skylet. He didn't know for sure. He couldn't. Nevertheless, he reached anyway.

The middle finger of his hand touched the scaly surface, but nothing happened. Oros began examining the texture of the cloak with his index finger and thumb. It felt slightly different than the one he wore, less rough. He could smell the dragon fire upon it, which seemed much more potent.

Letting the edge of the cloak go, Oros drew his attention back toward Skylet's face, which displayed some bruising and minimal cuts but was otherwise untouched. He studied it for a long while and soon recognized someone he hadn't seen since he was a boy, someone nearly forgotten: he saw the face of his mother. His father's too, though from that angle, there was no mistaking the young woman before him was his kin.

He started to cry again, reaching his bruised and battered hand to touch her smooth face. A warm sensation emanated from her, soothing his sore extremity.

He quickly recoiled his hand and covered his face with both palms as he allowed the emotions to flow, racing back through everything he had done to her in his blind quest to find the dragon. The fact that Jessie and Séya had been captured, probably tortured by soldiers, made him feel even worse. He was doubtful as he came back to himself and the present time that Skylet would be reasonable if she were awake. Still, he felt responsible and wanted to set it right.

He reached into his pouch and pulled out the vial of Dragon's Blood, twisted open the cap, and proceeded to pour drops over her deepest wounds first. Since she lost a great deal of her vital fluid, Oros was worried about how much strength she would have whenever she woke up.

There was a sizzling sound that came from the places where the Dragon's Blood had been dropped. Oros watched as the flesh of Skylet's wounds slowly began reconnecting. He used his fingers and dabbed traces of the blood on the less severe injuries and cuts on her body. Soon, she was all healed, nary a cut or scratch could be found on her, but still she lay motionless on the ground.

Oros put the vial back in his pouch and sat with his legs crossed. He removed his weapons and placed them in front of himself, and then he waited for any sign of movement.

Before long, Skylet's body began twitching. Oros didn't move. He seemed remarkably calm. Her arms and legs stirred and in moments, Skylet slowly opened her eyes to find Oros sitting in front of her with his eyes closed. Startled to see him, and even more so by his scarred appearance, she staggered to her feet and stepped back from him, nearly tripping backward as she tried to regain her strength. Skylet looked down at herself, stroked her face and neck and realized that her wounds were gone. It was as if she hadn't been touched. There was silence between the two.

"Pick your weapon," Oros said softly, his eyes still closed.

"What?" she asked.

"Pick your weapon."

"Where is Séya?"

"Pick your weapon, and I will reveal that to you."

Skylet cautiously walked toward him and picked up a knife. The same knife he threateningly held to her before at the old soldier encampment. "Fine," she said. "I have a knife. Now, where is she?"

"The soldiers took her and the dragon away."

"Then you will take me to them. Now!" Skylet demanded.

"Let me tell you about your mother first," Oros said.

Skylet blinked. "Jessie raised me. She is my mother."

"Yes, but she didn't bear you."

"We are wasting time!" Skylet shouted. "You will take me to them now or I will stab you!" She stormed over to him and held the knife to his neck.

Oros didn't flinch. He sat as calm as ever, eyes still closed. "Your face is like hers," Oros began. "She was gentle and fierce when she needed to be."

Skylet stayed herself with the knife to Oros's neck, shaking.

"She used to sing to my baby sister," he said. "I didn't want to leave her, but I was training to be a Dragonhunter. And all these years," he slowly opened his eyes, looking away from her at first. "I thought my sister was dead. Burned to ash with our parents while I was away." His eyes slowly found hers, tears still streaming.

Skylet had the knife to his neck and slowly began to lower it. She looked into his eyes, beyond his cuts and burns and saw a man in pain. A shred of pity tapped her heart before she pushed it aside.

"Ereyan," Oros said. "That was your given name at birth."

Skylet stood before Oros and then stepped back. She began to understand what was being explained to her, though she couldn't feel any connection. The man before her was still a stranger.

She turned away from him and stood, her back facing him. Processing what she had just learned, Skylet began walking away and then quickly turned to face him. "You're not my brother," she said sharply. "I had a brother, and you killed him."

"I make no excuses for my actions," Oros said softly. "But kill him, I did not."

"I don't believe you, liar" she spat. "Wearing his skin

like a trophy." Skylet gestured to the cloak he wore.

Oros looked down at the article wrapped about him. "Your brother was strong," he said. "We fought heartily."

"Quiet yourself! Don't speak about him to me!"

"He was different from any other dragon I faced. The fire in his spirit, I could almost touch."

"I should kill you right now!" Skylet raced toward him quickly and held the knife to Oros's neck firmly. The slightest movement from either of them would draw blood.

He continued to sit. "We battled until neither of us could stand to strike; I held his hand, and he held mine as he died." Oros released a deep sigh. "He was my greatest opponent."

"Quiet!"

Oros persisted. He was cleansing himself. "I stayed with him for days following his death. The cloak is a reminder of his courage and his spirit."

Skylet screamed and kicked Oros with all her might. He keeled over on his side, then she jumped on top of him and raised the knife, looking at Oros's face.

"You have my deepest apologies," he said. "You will find the dragon and the woman in Selnes's largest encampment for soldiers at the center of town." Then he closed his eyes and relaxed his body.

Skylet's eyes were so full of tears that they blurred her vision of Oros, who lay seemingly comfortable under her weight. She held the knife above her but began to wonder why, the impulse to stab Oros long gone.

Dropping her arms to her sides, Skylet let out a deep sigh and cried into her arm. She got off of Oros and stood over him.

He opened his eyes and looked at her face, wet from

sweat and tears.

"Show me the encampment," she said to him.

27.

The two walked in silence for a long time. Oros led the way while Skylet remained a few feet behind. Both of them hooded beneath their cloaks, neither could look at each other much less speak.

They came through the forest and back past the battle area where now much of the formerly green grass, trees, and homes had been reduced to charred ashes.

They walked past where Skylet had fallen almost to her doom when she felt her pouches, realizing that one was missing something. She gasped to herself, not realizing that Oros heard.

"What is it?" he asked.

"Nothing," Skylet responded sharply, half scanning the area as she walked.

Oros stopped and watched her looking around the ground when he realized that he might know what it was she was searching for.

He reached into his pouch and pulled out the vial of Dragon's Blood. "Are you searching for this?" he asked, holding it out to her.

"How did you find that," she asked, snatching the item from him.

"I found it around here before I began to search for you. You must have dropped it when you fled."

She examined the vial and noticed that some of the blood was missing. Skylet started to ask him if he had used any, then she remembered the burns and scars, which he still had.

Seemingly reading her thoughts, Oros spoke. "You had deep wounds that required care," he said, turning from her and continuing to move forward.

Skylet looked herself over quickly as she moved. She didn't want to thank him. As far as she was concerned, after kidnapping her, throwing her over a railing, and fighting with Arca killing him or not, there was no way for Oros to make amends.

They traveled far from the battlefield and through a vast meadow, noticing groups of people huddling amongst each other, whispering words like *dragon* and *witch*.

Skylet was brought back to the moment from her heavy thoughts to hear the bystanders. Her heart pounded as she felt nothing good from the ways the people of Selnes spoke about her family.

They went along until they saw in the distance, near the top of a large mound, a towering, long granite building.

"There," Oros said as they stopped to look. "That is the main encampment of Selnes."

They would have to go through an area of homes, markets, and other buildings before they could get there. Oros and Skylet noticed many people were all walking in the direction of the station.

"They are all headed to the square," said Oros. "Perhaps to watch as your friend burns. We must move quickly."

With that, the two hastened their pace, moving past groups of people who were going in the same direction but were detouring to the right, as the main square was farther down, past the encampment.

Skylet was afraid for Jessie and Séya, her mind journeying to the most horrible of places. She just hoped that they would still be alive by the time she and Oros reached them.

28.

Séya awoke to darkness. A thick sack covered her face. She shook her head back and forth in an effort to remove it, but it was no use. She felt her arms and legs constrained in shackles, and after a few tries to break free, she gave up.

The room was cold. Séya could tell that she was in some sort of prison. The walls were cool brick with a few spaces where air was allowed in near the ceiling of the room. "Jessie," she whispered.

There was a shuffling sound coming from the ground to the right of her, joined by the clanking of chains. "Séya," said the dragon. She sounded weak.

"Thank goodness," the old woman let out a sigh of relief. "They haven't taken you away."

"I am still alive," Jessie said. "And, I still have my wings," she scoffed.

"Don't talk like that."

"The soldiers are coming for you, Séya," the dragon said.

Séya let out a quick guffaw that was muffled from the sack. "I'm not worried about them."

"I won't be able to protect you this time," Jessie said grimly.

Séya's mind wandered back to the battle and began wondering about Skylet's fate. "Where is Skylet?"

"I sent her away," Jessie said.

"Hm," Séya pondered. "Do you think she's safe?"

"I do," the dragon responded. "I know."

No more words were exchanged between the two.

Then came the faint and familiar sound of soldiers marching. As before, the marching came ominously closer and closer until finally, there was a loud thud at the door of the prison. The sound reverberated off the walls.

Séya and Jessie stayed quiet and waited. Soldiers clamored outside the old woman's cell, running the hilt of their weapons along the Moonbeam Metal bars, which caused Jessie to slowly coil her body toward herself.

One of the men opened the door to Séya's cell and sauntered in with supreme confidence. He was dark-haired, classically handsome. Having been a soldier for many years, it seemed he had waited ages for any sort of adventure. "Ready to burn, witch?" he asked, backhanding her in the face.

Jessie growled and staggered up. Without a thought, she slammed her large head against the bars of her cell that separated Séya from her.

The soldier turned to face Jessie, both of them staring swords into each other's faces. "Teach the dragon some manners," he shouted, not taking his eyes off of Jessie, who boldly returned his gaze.

Judging by how he spoke, Séya could tell that the man was a commander of the others. He seemed to revel in the power he possessed. Indeed, Commander Brawns was barely able to contain himself. She heard earnest footsteps and was afraid for her dear friend, her stomach clenching.

A soldier with a wooden staff stepped in to stick it through the bars and dug it into Jessie's wounds. Her cell was not nearly large enough for her to dodge the jabs.

The dragon howled and slammed her head against the bars again, putting a dent into them. Séya could feel the impact of Jessie's head deep in the core of herself.

"DON'T!" she cried. Her very heart felt as if it had been struck.

The footman kept sticking the dragon until she made ready to breathe fire. She inhaled, the inside of her mouth began to glow threateningly, but before she could exhale, another man threw his own wooden stick at the center of her throat, knocking her back against the brick wall behind her. The dragon yelped as the blood from her earlier wounds continued to stream slowly from her body, leaving traces on the rough stone floor. She keeled over on to her side, exhausted, and gingerly turned her head to see what was happening to Séya.

"You'll stay there," Brawns said, looking down at Jessie, her yellow-orange eyes glowing in the dim space. "Don't worry. You will have your turn to meet your fate," he said. "And it isn't what you think it will be."

The men in the room were huddled close together; they could feel the ground rumbling from the constant, low growling that came from Jessie.

Brawns turned away from the dragon and stepped up to Séya, snatching the dark sack from her face. She looked at him expressionless, as if he weren't there. The man grabbed her neck and stepped closer to her. "Look into my eyes, witch," Brawns said.

Séya did not comply.

Rather, she seemed to look beyond him. Commander

Brawns backhanded her again; punishment for not giving him the attention he so obviously deserved. "The herbs!" he called out.

Another soldier came to the front of the group and handed the commander a dirty, cream-colored pouch. He delicately untied the ribbon that kept it closed and dumped a small handful of finely ground herbs into his hand. The chains clanked as Séya shifted her position. Brawns noticed and paused, looking at Séya. "Good night," he said as he blew the herbs in her face.

Her body went limp almost immediately, the chains holding her in place. Brawns turned from her and made his way through the large group of men. "Unchain her and bring her to the square," he said.

They removed Séya from her bonds while Jessie watched helplessly as the soldiers began to clear the area. One of them carried the old woman over his shoulder and out of the prison room, the large door slamming behind him, echoing in the space with an emphasis that seemed almost final to Jessie.

Now, the dragon lay alone in the dark cell with only her thoughts and a shred of hope, which she wouldn't dare even whisper, that Séya would be okay.

29.

The men marched and chanted, excited that they had a witch in their custody. They were ready to show her off to an equally bloodthirsty mob of people. Farther away from the prison of the encampment they went, as spectators on the side cheered and chanted with them in near-perfect unison. "Death to the witch! Death to the witch!"

The soldiers moved along winding roads clanking their weapons on the ground and on the stonewall of nearby buildings.

Word quickly spread that there had been a dragon and a witch in the town of Selnes. As far as the townspeople were concerned, the witch conjured up the dragon. Possessing magical power was bad enough and was cause for Séya to die. Bringing a dragon to a place so sensitive to such creatures was even worse for her.

Soon, the men arrived at the open square. At the center, there stood the gallows with a noose hanging from a post. Residents had already reached the yard, waiting for the show to begin.

"What say you all?" yelled Commander Brawns as everyone began to settle in. "Should we burn the witch straight, or would you like to see a struggle?"

"She must struggle! Struggle!" one spectator shouted.

The soldiers and the bystanders laughed as the men carrying Séya marched up the stairs of the gallows and secured her limp body to the hanging post. The cheers were uproarious as Brawns walked up to the post and poured a bag of dark-colored dust in his hand. When he approached Séya, he extended his hand toward her cheek as if he might caress it, but instead, he threw the dust in her face. She started coughing and woke up to find herself bound to the hanging post. Her arms tied behind her back, her neck wrapped in a noose.

She looked around, noticing the many townspeople and all of the soldiers surrounding her. They stared with such a force that weighed on her. Before long, her emotions seemed to leave her under such public display, and then she felt nothing. They all looked like little more than a brick wall to her, and she stared into the heart of it.

"Have you any last words before you meet your end, witch?" asked Brawns.

Séya rolled her eyes in his direction and looked at his face, holding a blank gaze for a moment. Then she looked back at the wall of the crowd. "May you burn to ash and be claimed by the wind," she said.

The commander smiled wryly and raised his hand, signaling to one of the soldiers nearing the hanging lever to ready himself. He waited until the soldier was set; their eyes met, and Brawns dropped his hand.

The young soldier pulled the lever and the square floor space dropped beneath Séya's feet. Her body fell, and the rope straightened. The noose tightened itself around her neck as she hung there coughing and choking; the crowd cheered and screamed in excitement.

Séya swayed back and forth, struggling for air. Then suddenly, a spectator threw a flaming torch at the gallows, causing others to step back from the front. The torch narrowly missed Séya as she shook and floundered.

Two more flaming torches were hurled her way. One flew straight for her face; she could feel the heat brush past her as the torch went by. Then suddenly, there was a loud pop, and white smoke swiftly permeated the area. The spectators screamed and scattered about in the murky fog. "The witch is using black magic!" someone shouted.

"She has summoned evil spirits!" yelled another. Every which way, people ran and tumbled upon each other.

Amidst the commotion, coming from the thick of the fog, there were loud flapping sounds, like large flags being blown by a hard wind. Simultaneously, a fire began to catch against the base of the gallows. Just as Séya accepted her end, a sword cut through the rope, and she fell to the ground. Looking up from the dirt, Séya noticed the shapes of something she couldn't make out, clearing the smoke and fanning the flames about. It flapped and whipped around aggressively.

A mysterious hooded figure in a dark violet cloak made of dragon skin stepped beyond the flames and, through the thick haze, revealed herself to be Skylet. The cape flipped and swiped all around, throwing aside soldiers and spectators alike.

Ignited torches were sent Skylet's way, but she ducked low and allowed the cloak to guide her. She didn't fully understand how or why it behaved the way it did, seeming to sync itself to her movements and thoughts. It occurred to her that perhaps through her exposure to dragon blood earlier that some figurative door in the relationship between her and the cloak had opened, allowing for a conversation to take place.

She couldn't be sure and there was no time to ruminate on it. There were obstacles in her way and she needed to remove them.

Skylet twirled like a dancer, batting away the fiery sticks while sweeping would-be attackers off their feet.

Oros, meanwhile, took Séya from the gallows and carried her, running in a direction away from the commotion. Townspeople tried to stop him by attempting to tackle him, but he barreled over the small group and kept running. "Skylet!" he called out. "Let's go!"

She didn't respond.

Commander Brawns grabbed his sword and prepared to get up from the ground as waves of people poured over and around him, being swapped about by Skylet.

Still, more soldiers rushed toward her. Brawns walked deliberately to the girl amid all the commotion. His gaze remained trained on her. He got within feet of his target and immediately charged at full speed without a second thought. Like a prowling animal of the wild, he was silent, focused, and ready to inflict serious damage.

Brawns made to swing his sword toward her back, but Skylet turned around, and the edges of the cloak wrapped around his blade and forearm to flip him over onto his back, weapon tossed aside.

The other end of the cape was quickly coming down to cover him, but he rolled out of the way.

The cloak raised itself high above Skylet, somehow getting longer than it actually was.

Brawns looked up as it towered above him threateningly, like some large creature for a few seconds before the tips of the cloak became as sharp as daggers, and quickly darted after him.

He boldly jumped toward Skylet and was close enough to strike her with his fist, but as he took a swing, the left lower edge of the cloak swooped in and cut his forearm, though he quickly turned and got low enough to trip Skylet with a sweep of his foot.

She flipped over, and the hooded garment broke her fall, allowing her to recover and land feet first.

Skylet made a quick swiping motion with her hand and the cloak, mimicking this movement, sliced him across his face. Brawns growled in pain and twisted away, noticing his sword in the distance.

Skylet was beginning to feel more comfortable with the cloak and its movements as it worked to protect her. "Where is she?" Skylet asked Brawns forcefully.

He pulled out a long knife and rushed toward the girl, swiping and slashing with precision and skill, though he never actually touched her.

The cloak flopped around, expanding and contracting to block the attacks. They kept at it until the cape wrapped around his arm and wrestled him to the ground. He struggled hard, but the cloak became too much for him. Lying on his back, tightly bundled in the garment, Skylet questioned him again. "Where is she?"

"The dragon is my prisoner," Brawns spat, gasping for air.

"You will tell me where she is," unbeknownst to Skylet, large thorns slowly began protruding from the cloak moving closer and closer to his neck.

"You'll have to— kill me," he said, struggling.

"Is that what you want?" Skylet asked, her voice low and serious.

The thorns touched his neck and kept going, piercing his skin, slowly going deeper. He screamed in pain, struggling to break free of the cloak, but it just got tighter as the thorns went deeper.

"I won't stop until you tell me," Skylet said. "Or, actually. . ." she trailed off. Reaching into her pouch, she pulled out the container of Dragon's Blood and poured some of it into her hand. She put the vial away and rubbed her palms together, kneeling over him. When the thorns from the cloak retracted themselves, Skylet applied the Dragon's Blood to the commander's neck, and soon his deep wounds healed. "Next time, I won't be so merciful," said Skylet. "You will tell me where she is, or you will die."

The two of them delivered hardened stares at one another. It was as if the commotion surrounding them was non-existent.

"All right!" Brawns exclaimed through a cough. "I'll tell you. . ."

"You will tell me, and you will take me there," Skylet demanded.

30.

Oros carried Séya deep into the forest, away from the square, and placed her at the foot of an oak tree. He took out his knife and cut the ropes tied around her wrists; then, he helped her remove the noose from her neck. She looked up at him stoically and said nothing.

"Are you all right?" he asked her.

She didn't respond. Instead, she looked away from him.

"I can only imagine what you think of me," said Oros through a deep sigh. "I am changed."

"And why should I believe you?" Séya asked.

"You shouldn't," responded Oros. "And yet, I speak true."

The silence was thick between them.

Oros looked away.

"I found that girl when she was a baby," Séya began.

Oros slowly turned to face her as she sat at the foot of the tree, staring off beyond where he stood.

Séya looked as if she could see the memory of finding Skylet playing somewhere off in the distance. "I think of that night often, when I took her out of the water and calmed her as she cried."

Oros listened intently and knelt across from her so that he was at her eye level.

"I watched her mature into the beautiful and kind young woman she is today, and you have scarred her."

"Yes," he said. "I have."

"I should curse you now," Séya said. "Finish what the fire started with your face."

"I want you to. I will not fight," said Oros softly. "Before you do, we must go back."

"For what? So you can kill Jessie?" Séya replied, getting to her feet, leaning her back against the tree to get her bearings.

"No," Oros replied. "The dragon showed me. . ." He paused.

"Well?" Séya shot back.

Oros looked up at Séya's face. She held his gaze; there was a softness the old woman noticed while looking at his burned features that she hadn't seen before.

"She is my sister," he said.

"What?" Séya asked in surprise. She looked down to the ground and slowly realized that the hunter was genuine.

"It is true," Oros said. "I thought she was dead all these years, burned alive with my parents."

Séya took a moment to process everything she was hearing. "And where is she?" asked Séya.

"Back near the gallows," replied Oros. "I called for her, but she was fighting. Her cloak. . ."

"Her cloak," Seya repeated. "Jessie and I made sure that she would be protected by it should her life ever be in danger."

"I knew it had to be magical," Oros said almost to himself.

"But she didn't. We never told her."

"Why?"

"Because we wanted her to value her life and not believe she was invincible."

"She's going after the dragon," Oros said. "There are soldiers with Moonbeam Metal there. We must go back."

Séya stood straighter, regaining some of her strength. She looked at Oros, who was still kneeling on the ground, and let out a deep sigh.

"Then let us go," she said.

31.

Skylet held Commander Brawns hostage as he led her to the main encampment at the center of Selnes. The cloak wrapped around his neck loose enough so that he could still breathe and speak. "She's here, right?" Skylet asked him.

Brawns gave her a strained nod.

They went in through the large, heavy wooden doors and were quickly approached by many soldiers. "Sir!" one of them exclaimed as he rushed toward Skylet with his sword. Others followed suit and brought out their respective weapons. There were men located in higher balcony areas with arrows and spears trained on the girl.

"Stay back!" Skylet shouted, her voice echoing throughout the large hall. "Stay back, or he dies!"

"Kill. . . her!" Brawns said through a cackle.

Three of the soldiers in the upper wings fired arrows at her. A split second before they were to strike Skylet, the other end of the cloak that was not wrapped around the commander's neck reached out and batted them away. The mantle tightened around him and forced the man to his knees.

"I've come for the dragon," Skylet said. "You will release her to me, and we will leave peacefully."

The room was silent.

"Tell them to drop their weapons," Skylet demanded.

Brawns did not comply.

So she raised her right hand slowly, and the cloak mimicked her, pulling the commander up by his neck.

His body suspended from the floor, he waved his hands downward, signaling for the soldiers to drop their weapons. The cacophonous sound of metal clanked as the weaponry fell to the stone floor.

"Now," she said, lowering her voice for Brawns. "Take me to her." She put him down, the cloak still wrapped around his neck.

They continued to walk through the large bottom floor of the encampment until they reached a door to the far right of the room. Brawns tried to gather his keys, but Skylet grabbed them out of a pouch at his waist and proceeded to unlock the door herself. He pushed it open, and the two of them walked through. The corridor was dark, even in the daylight. There were windows, but not enough sunlight came in to consider the space well lit. It was also cold, but Skylet didn't think about that. All she could think of was Jessie.

They reached another door made of iron and opened it. Down another corridor, they travelled, reaching a point beyond which there was a hallway. A brick wall stood only feet ahead of them where there was a square shaped opening in the ceiling that was barred, the only source of light for many feet in either direction of the hallway. "Left or right?" she asked him.

Brawns gestured to the right, and so they went, all the

way to the back where they reached a set of massive double doors made of steel.

Skylet unlocked them by removing a rod that kept them closed, then she and Brawns pushed it open. Slowly, they moved into the large space of a prison. As they walked around the various empty box-shaped cells, Skylet sensed the dragon. She knew immediately that Jessie was there somewhere, but was she alive?

At last, they reached the area where Jessie was. Brawns pointed to the large cell where the dragon lay coiled up like a wounded dog. Though it was large, it was almost too small for Jessie. Skylet wondered how such a massive captive was fit into the tight space. Something was off about what Skylet saw. Jessie didn't seem to be moving or even breathing. "Jessie," she said softly.

It took a moment, but the dragon began to shuffle and attempted to sit up. "Dear child," she said. "I am glad you are safe." The relief in her voice comforted the girl.

"I'm here to take you home," said Skylet. She saw the blood beneath Jessie and something that looked like a tube attached to where one of her wounds was. Blood was being drained into a large jar nearby.

"What are you doing to her?" Skylet asked Brawns, the cloak's grip tightened. She didn't allow him to answer. "You will not have her blood." She slammed his face into the bars of the cell twice and then tossed him aside where he lay motionless. Skylet took the keys and unlocked the prison door, slowly stepping inside Jessie's cell. Her hands gently caressed the dragon's bruised face.

"I see the cloak has taken good care of you," the dragon smiled slightly.

"I don't understand it," Skylet said.

"You don't have to. It does," Jessie explained. "It understands a threat to your life and responds. Séya and I wanted to make sure you were safe even when we weren't around," Jessie explained.

"How?"

The dragon shrugged her shoulders and looked away.

"So it *is* magical," said Skylet.

"We hoped it would never be used," the dragon explained. "It is a part of you now and will protect you always."

Skylet took in the information and suddenly began to worry about what Jessie said. "Are you able to move?" she asked.

"Just barely," the dragon said.

"Come on, let's go home."

"I'm in too much pain to fly, girl," said the dragon.

"We have to get out before the other soldiers get here, Jessie."

"Skylet," the dragon said solemnly, reaching out and touching her shoulder. "Find Séya and go home."

Skylet understood what that meant; it felt very final, but she disregarded it. "I won't leave you here," said Skylet. "We have to get out now!" She began tugging at the dragon's rough arm.

"Come here, child," said the dragon softly. She gently pulled Skylet close and studied her. From her feet all the way up to her face, she looked and stared into the girl's eyes, her breathing irregular. "You still have so much anger in you," the dragon said. "Fear too." She touched Skylet's face with her hand. "Let me show you something." She leaned her head against Skylet's, and then suddenly, a vision appeared.

Skylet saw a man and a woman looking down at her, smiling and touching her gently. The feeling was one of warmth, comfort, and safety. A boy appeared and looked into the crib, where Skylet gazed up at him, arms raised. The boy was serious, but his energy felt comforting to her. She recognized him as Oros. Skylet felt herself shaking in disbelief. She grappled with a range of emotions when she looked at his smooth and almost cherubic face. A mix of intense excitement from within her infant self and near-unbridled anger from her present self sat at odds inside her as she relived the memory. Yet, there it was, impossible for her to deny.

Young Oros leaned over the crib to kiss her forehead before turning to leave at the sound of another man.

The next thing Skylet saw was the warm and glowing face of a woman she understood to be her mother, as she was picked up and showered with kisses.

The woman's golden brown skin seemed blessed by the very essence of the sun. Light in the room from candles caressed the surface of her face like a silk veil, and her dense, dark hair made up of loose curls dropped neatly just past her shoulders. Skylet was genuinely stunned by the sight of her mother, whose name she knew deep within herself: Gailia.

Among everything she tried to take in while occupying the memory, it was the woman's eyes that Skylet found most striking. Almond-shaped with sharp edges, and an endlessly deep brown like hers, like Séya's too. It surprised Skylet how much she saw of the sorceress in the face of the woman before her. She believed strongly that her mother would have gotten along well with Séya and Jessie.

A sudden, loud crash disrupted the tender moment,

causing everything to rumble. The girl's mother went outside with her father, still carrying her, and noticed that there were fires all over the town.

A large dragon in the distance was laying waste to everything in its path; the commotion made the baby cry uncontrollably. Soon, the home was torn to shreds by the dragon's tail slamming into it.

Skylet saw herself being lowered into a wicker basket, and then she saw darkness. Shaking within the vessel, she heard the screams of people running by attempting to evade the danger. For others, it was too late. They scrambled around, burning from all the dragon fire.

The lid was opened, and Skylet saw her beautiful mother, with tears in her eyes, burns on her neck and arms. Gailia planted many kisses upon her child's face before closing the basket and placing it in the water. Skylet felt a pang in her heart, longing for a final embrace, like the dream of a warm home-cooked meal.

When the basket top opened again, Skylet saw the face of someone she knew very well. It was Séya, the old woman with a kind face.

The vision faded and was over. Both Jessie and Skylet had tears in their eyes. "Absolve yourself of anger," said the dragon. "Be filled, now, with love and forgiveness. Or try to be."

"Jessie," Skylet said.

"Promise me you'll try," said the dragon slowly.

Skylet stood for a moment, looking into the face of Jessie. It was the first time she really saw the dragon's radiance. Rarely had she thought much about that before, yet, as she took in the bloody scratches around Jessie's features, it seemed so clear, even in such a poorly lit place.

The girl exhaled deeply. "He almost killed me."

Jessie gave Skylet a look that was pleading and touched her very core.

"Jessie. . ." the girl trailed off in a whisper. She knew there was no way her words would be the definitive end on the matter.

The dragon looked at her and said nothing. She just observed and saw both the baby Séya had introduced her to and the young woman standing across from her. There was a space of calm between the two of them where it seemed nothing else, and no one else was around. They listened to each other's breathing and took in the stillness.

It was a moment not unlike the time they spent upon the mountain in Quentanan just days before. A lifetime ago, it seemed to Skylet. As she thought of that day, she wanted nothing more than to go back and stay there. Yet neither that time in The Sky nor the moment she found herself in at present, could last forever. No matter how much either of them might have wanted it to. "All right," Skylet said with reluctance. "I will."

"I love you, Skylet."

"Jessie come, let's go home. Please."

The dragon wrapped her arms and wings around Skylet as best she could, and held her lovingly. Skylet squeezed with all her strength, tears streaming down her face. "I love you," said Skylet.

The dragon breathed deeply twice and then she didn't breathe anymore. Her body went limp and slid to the floor.

Something fell out of Jessie's hand and bounced on to the ground. Skylet looked down to see the yellow-orange pin from her cloak. She picked it up and held it tightly in her hand, standing for a moment to take in the fact that

Jessie was no longer moving, and then she knelt and cried against Jessie's face.

Skylet was allowed a short space of time, which she did her best to savor until the dragon's body began to glow, and then it lit up like a bright lamp. Skylet leaned aside to take in as much of the sight as she could. Her eyes widened as the large body began to twinkle like a star before turning to a glittery silver dust that rose from the ground and wrapped around her before allowing itself to be absorbed by the cloak she wore. It glowed momentarily before going back to its dark violet color.

Now, she was alone in the prison cell. A thought reached her that took her away from her emotions for a moment, which was to take the large jar of Jessie's blood so that soldiers couldn't use it. She stood up, thinking only of the jar and took a step toward it.

Commander Brawns began to stir from his place on the floor of the prison. He turned his head and saw Skylet standing over the jar, looking down at it. His face contorted in confusion as he realized the large dragon was gone. Careful not to alert Skylet to the fact that he had come to, he stayed low and quietly made his way toward the cell where the girl was.

She bent down to reach for the jar, but before she could touch it, Brawns had suddenly lunged at her from behind with a large hunting knife. Just as the blade was about to make contact, the cloak came alive and reflexively wrapped around him. He struggled terribly, grabbing and stabbing at the cape as hard as he could, but the knife never penetrated.

Just before he took his last strained breath, he saw a

pair of yellow-orange eyes scowling at him in the darkness. When he stopped moving, the cloak released him, letting his body plop onto the solid stone floor.

32.

Séya and Oros were close to the encampment entrance when they stopped just before reaching the pathway leading to the front door. They stayed out of sight, hiding among bushes. "There are too many soldiers outside," said Séya. "I don't have the energy for a big spell to remove them all right now."

Oros went into his pouch and pulled out a small bag. "My last one," he said. "It'll have to do to create enough of a diversion to get us inside."

Séya straightened herself and prepared to move out. "I have an idea," she said. "Toss it out, and we'll use the smoke as cover as we move."

"It's the best plan we have," Oros said, releasing a deep breath. "Whenever you're ready."

Séya took a moment to herself and quickly turned to Oros. "Now," she said.

Oros tossed out the white bag, and when it hit the ground, it exploded. The two of them quickly ran out from the bushes and into the fog.

"Stay close," Seya said. She began waving her hands as if she were engaged in a dance. Using her magic, she guided the fog that covered and surrounded them as they moved closer to the front door of the encampment. The men scurried about in confusion. Some, in an attempt to get out from under the fog and see more clearly, ran into Oros and Séya.

They tried to attack, but Oros took down two of them. A third was slightly more trouble for him, but after Oros cut him in the shoulder with his sword, subduing him was easier.

The large doors to the station creaked open, and soldiers poured out. Through the fog, they came. Séya steadily tried to move the cloud along with them, but she had to stop occasionally, using a spell to knock out a soldier or two. They were deep into the center of the main room of the encampment now.

Arrows zinged all around them.

"Get down!" shouted Oros.

Séya crouched with him and kept moving forward. "Skylet!" Séya shouted. It was impossible to hear any single voice clearly with the level of commotion taking place inside.

They continued to move until Oros was struck in the leg by an arrow. He yelped in pain and fell to the floor but tried to continue his steady pace, shuffling forward. Séya stopped to check on him, and suddenly an arrow struck her shoulder. She screamed and waved the opposite hand at the place where it stuck out, resulting in the projectile removing itself from her shoulder. However, no sooner than she got rid of it did another sharply graze her stomach. She keeled over in pain, falling to her knees.

Oros and Séya found themselves quickly surrounded by numerous men who were rushing in. The hunter tried to defend himself, blocking sword attacks from some of the soldiers, but he was no match for all of them. Two soldiers stabbed him in the back and arm. He fell face forward on the ground.

Séya had slightly better luck moving soldiers out of the way, but her magic was weakened because of her low energy. A particularly agile soldier moved toward her like a shadow, intent on taking Séya's head clean off. His sword made it a hair away from her neck before he was picked up from the ground and thrown far away. Séya couldn't tell what forces were at work because the fog was still too thick.

Soldiers were suddenly flying every which way, followed by what sounded like a whip. The men cleared the area surrounding Oros and Séya quickly, not understanding at all what was happening. "It's another dragon!" one shouted. "Run!"

"It is a demon!" shouted another.

A silhouette of what looked like Skylet could be seen through the fog. She walked with purpose through the wave of soldiers, occasionally sidestepping and twisting around them. She held the jar of Jessie's blood as her cloak reacted, flapping and grabbing at the men. Some of the footmen tried to attack her, while others, not knowing what to do, scattered around. When she reached Séya on the floor, she knelt and placed the jar beside her.

"Dear child," Séya said, relieved. She reached out her hand and wiped a tear from Skylet's face. She knew something was wrong, but wasn't sure exactly what.

Meanwhile, the soldiers kept coming, and the cloak kept defending against them. It took a moment, but Séya understood suddenly what Skylet knew and felt in her soul.

The cape abruptly expanded beyond anything Séya could imagine, and in that instant, she felt as if an old friend was fighting beside her, protecting her again. "Jessie," Séya said almost under her breath, tears forming in her eyes. The old woman clutched her chest feeling the connection she once did just before she met the dragon.

Skylet just looked at Séya; the two of them shared a rich silence only they understood. The girl stood up and took three steps away from Séya, standing in the center. She knelt and closed her eyes. The cloak removed itself from Skylet and now acted as an entity completely separate from her. It expanded to a dome shape a third of the size of the large room in the encampment and covered Séya, Oros, and Skylet in a protective shield.

The garment then began to close in, tightening the shell so that there was only enough room for the three of them. It was effectively dark inside the dome. Séya turned and placed her hand against its surface. "My dear friend, we need light," she said softly. The inside of the cloak began to glow a muted violet color until they all could see each other again. Through the rumblings and sounds outside of the dome they shared a moment of calm.

Skylet stood up and walked over to the jar of Jessie's blood. She opened it and reached her hand inside, putting her bloody palm on Séya's wounds. Slowly, they began to heal.

"Thank you, child," she said.

Skylet went back to the jar and put her hand inside once more to collect blood. She walked over to Oros, who lay motionless on his stomach, faintly breathing. Skylet saw the extent of his wounds and knelt first to heal the injury in Oros's back. She then smeared blood on the puncture his leg sustained before turning him over to see his face. His eyes were closed, looking almost as if he were sleeping. Yet, he didn't look peaceful. He seemed to be having a bad dream.

She went back to the jar of Jessie's blood and scooped out some more. When she got back to Oros, she stood over him, looking at his damaged face, Jessie's blood dripping from her hands. The girl took a deep breath and then knelt beside him, placing her hands on his face. She began rubbing the blood all over, covering his features and neck in the way a nurse might. Soon, his wounds and burns began to heal. "I forgive you," she said quietly, not knowing whether he heard her or if she even believed what she said.

"We should leave now," Séya gently chimed in. She heard scratches and banging outside the dome from all around.

The soldiers tried to get in using their swords. After many attempts, an arrow had finally pierced the cloak and bounced off the ground, narrowly missing Skylet's shoulder. She wasn't afraid.

Instead, she stood up calmly and walked toward Séya. Taking the old woman's hand, she noticed even through the traces of Jessie's drying blood covering her palm that it felt surprisingly like a smooth sheet considering everything it had endured. They walked toward Oros, who was still lying on the ground, his breathing returning to normal. He began to stir, waking up after a moment or two.

Meanwhile, swords and other weapons began breaching the cloak dome, holes ripping through the surface. Skylet and Séya huddled over Oros, who was now awake, their heads all touching. The girl drew a deep breath and exhaled. The magical garment quickly broke its dome formation and returned to Skylet's shoulders. She raised her hand and moved it in a circular motion above her head; the bottom of the cloak extended and quickly mimicked her motion, whipping around in a wide ring to subdue the enemies.

"Let's go!" shouted Séya. They all ran through the large front doors, exiting the encampment. Séya turned and mumbled something quickly, placing her palms together, and the front doors swiftly slammed themselves shut.

The three of them ran past the injured bodies of a few soldiers and into the woods nearby.

33.

They carried on, none of them knowing where they might rest.

"There's a river coming up," shouted Oros. "Straight ahead!"

They ran and soon emerged from the woods only to come upon large rocks high above the water. Leaning against boulders and oak trees, they rested themselves for a moment. "We need to keep moving," said Oros. "More soldiers are coming for us."

There was no response. Séya and Skylet held each other and cried together. Oros stood by silently.

He felt awkward, wanting to provide some comfort, but not knowing how. Oros walked up to them as they knelt on the ground, overcome with grief. The most honest thing he thought to do was to join them. He dropped to one knee, reaching out to touch both of them, one hand on either of their shoulders. "We must leave," he said softly.

Séya took a breath and exhaled. "Which way?" she asked, sniffling.

"We move south," he said.

Just then, he heard a snap of twigs in the distance. Someone was near. Suddenly, Skylet's cloak pushed Oros backward and Séya to the side. An arrow flew from the forest directly at Skylet, but the mantle reached out and batted it away. As she stepped forward to prepare herself for another fight, a host of twenty soldiers emerged from the woods, their weapons drawn. "Surrender," one of them demanded. "You've nowhere else to run."

"Archers! Fire!" shouted another soldier.

"Wait!" The first soldier turned back in an effort to stop the archers, but it was too late. A swarm of projectiles, already released, flew toward Skylet. She quickly turned and ran for the edge of the rocks, jumping over. The ends of her cloak reached back and grabbed Oros and Séya, taking them down with her.

The arrows narrowly missed as she fell into the river. On the way down, the cloak detached from Skylet and re-formed itself into a cup-shaped boat that broke Skylet's fall. She and Séya landed in the center of the small vessel while Oros was nowhere to be found. Still, they moved in the direction the current took them, which was traveling downstream.

Skylet looked back into the water and still saw nothing. Arrows flew toward them, and Séya managed to redirect some of the projectiles back, striking archers in the arms or legs.

Oros emerged from the rapidly moving current. He swam with all his strength to catch up to the boat.

While swimming, his mind took him back to the water training sessions with his uncle, the least favorite type of training for him. Servalan tried to teach him about fighting a dragon on or near water. "A good hunter is skilled at engaging a dragon on land," he would say, "but a great one could engage in water as well."

One had to be an advanced swimmer to stand a chance against some dragons, as the creatures could move as quickly in water as they could on land or in the air. Oros would swim behind the small boat Servalan steered in lively waters as large bags of sand were thrown out. Contraptions that shot fire in different forms were employed to present obstacles for the boy to overcome.

It took many, many tries, more than he would ever admit to anyone. Eventually, he caught up and made his way to the boat.

He came back to himself and realized as he struggled to catch up to Skylet and Séya, that this time was not so different. Only no one was ever shooting arrows at him before. He worried that he couldn't make it, yet Oros swam with everything left inside himself. Against the flow of water that pulsed with the force of a blazing fire, he was swallowed by the current more than once only to reemerge at the surface, slamming into rocks, trying to keep steady.

Still he swam as other archers continued to fire. Getting close once more, this time, Skylet reached her hand out for him. He grabbed hold as the river turned into a waterfall.

They all went over the edge, Skylet and Oros losing each other's hands in the process, landing into an area of calm water out of reach of the soldiers. Skylet and Séya frantically looked around for Oros as the boat slowly moved along the water, but he was gone. The two shared a concerned look. Séya reached out to carefully take Skylet's hands and hold them as they sat in the stillness of the water.

After a few moments, the old woman pulled Skylet in

for a hug and they sat quietly together. There had been too much loss for one day, and now they needed to figure out how to manage their grief for both Jessie and Oros.

Suddenly, the water stirred behind them. Séya and Skylet looked in the direction they came from to see what looked to be Oros's cloak floating in the water. The two of them looked on and after a moment, he emerged from the water, dramatically filling his lungs with air. Oros looked around quickly for the boat to find Skylet and Séya waving for him to catch up.

"Come on!" Skylet shouted.

He grabbed his cape and began swimming toward them, his strokes labored. Finally, he climbed onto the boat.

"Are you all right?" Séya asked, helping him get settled.

"I will live," replied Oros, catching his breath. "Thank you."

The three of them sat quietly together as they got used to the stillness of the water.

34.

They traveled in silence for what seemed like hours. Séya used light magic to propel them along. In the distance, a sandy beach gave way to tall rocky cliffs. Skylet felt something in her stomach, though she didn't know what it was. As they moved closer to the beach, the feeling became stronger within her. "Let's stop there," Skylet said. "Séya, can you push us there?"

Séya made sure they reached the beach using her magic. They got out of the cloak boat and stepped on to the sand. The cape returned to its normal state and draped itself around Skylet.

"What is it, child?"

"I don't know," replied Skylet. "I feel something."

They walked along the beach until they came to a hole in a tall cliff wall. It was large enough to fit at least two people through at the same time.

Skylet walked up to the base of the hole and began climbing the large rocks to get to it. As the feeling within her became stronger, the cloak reacted, becoming noticeably warmer and flapping minimally. Skylet reached the opening and entered.

"Skylet!" Séya called out. She climbed the rocks and

followed the girl inside, Oros close behind.

Skylet took a few steps inside the cavern and felt a cool breeze circulating through the space. The deeper they moved, the darker it got. Skylet moved quickly as she climbed over rocks and logs. Finally, she reached a point deep in the cave that she could barely make out. Yet, she didn't feel she needed to go any farther. Her cape bordered on hot now, and though she began to sweat, Skylet was too preoccupied with where she was for the heat to bother her. She knelt and started shifting twigs, dirt, and rocks around.

"What is it you're looking for?" asked Oros.

Skylet didn't answer. She kept searching as though no one was there.

Séya then got down on her knees and moved rocks around. She began moving heaps of dirt and twigs away until she felt the surface of something smooth. Upon first glance, it looked like a rock. A tremor of heat rushed through her body.

She paused and became gentler with how she dug around the polished surface of the rock. Séya continued until she saw that what lay before her was revealed to be a large dragon egg. Once it was fully exposed, they all took a moment to look at it. Séya cautiously picked it up and held it, cupping it like a most rare and valuable gem. "Let us go," she said softly.

They traveled back to the beach and sat in a circle surrounding the dragon egg. It was a warm afternoon at that point, and they decided to sit in the sun for a while and figure out what to do next.

"Oh, I was beginning to think I would never see another egg intact," Séya said, trying to contain her excitement. "Jessie's spirit is with us. She brought us here."

Skylet looked over at Séya, who was marveling at the egg. The old woman's eyes slowly found Skylet looking back at her. She stood and stepped over to the young woman she had watched grow up, the two looking into each other's eyes. Skylet rose, and they embraced tightly, overcome with emotion.

Oros stood and watched before turning to survey the ocean.

Séya leaned back to look at Skylet's face, the two still holding each other. "Do you know," Séya began, sniffling as she spoke. "Jessie taught me a deeper understanding of my abilities?"

Skylet slowly shook her head. It wasn't until that moment that she ever considered a time Séya never understood her own power. She always assumed the old woman knew what to do, knew who she was at all times.

"In my youth, I was rejected by most everyone, but Jessie cared for me."

Skylet scanned the old woman's face, and as they clutched each other, she could see, she could feel Séya as a young woman in a way that was different from how she seemed usually. She saw a woman who was lost and uncertain about her future. She could see the hope Jessie gave to the old woman and the love her heart carried for the dragon.

"It was through Jessie sharing her spirit, her love, and her magic with me, that I began to understand my own." Séya cupped Skylet's face and held it lovingly, removing the trail of tears with her thumbs.

The girl nestled her head into Séya's shoulder and allowed herself to cry hard. Séya held her as tight as she could. "I'm going to miss her too," said Séya, her voice trembling. The old woman closed her eyes and allowed her tears to fall.

Séya's mind wandered to waking up in the cave on the day Jessie saved her from the townspeople at Crescent Lake so many years ago. She saw the dragon bowing to her in her mind's eye and felt comforted.

Séya thought of how often the two sat across from each other on the grass in the center of the cave. Many long days were spent silently communing, getting to know and understand one another. The adventures they shared, the dragon eggs they found, all the memories rushed back to her as she held Skylet, in much the same way that Jessie once held the old woman.

An abrupt cracking sound suddenly jolted Séya out of her thoughts. No one paid any attention to it at first. It wasn't until they heard more of the same noise that everyone looked at the egg and noticed a breach in the surface of the shell.

Séya and Skylet released each other and slowly knelt to be at eye level of the egg. Oros turned to witness what was happening, but he didn't move.

It wasn't much longer before the shell fell apart, and a small, frail baby-blue-colored dragon revealed itself. It made soft squawking sounds, its arms, and legs flapping every which way.

"Ulonae," Skylet said.

"What?" asked Séya.

"Her name is Ulonae."

Séya gave Skylet a quizzical look. "How do you know

that name?" she asked.

Skylet shrugged her shoulders. "I think Jessie gave it to me," replied Skylet. She began to understand the cloak's influence more. "The name of the dragon who brought me to you and Jessie when I was a baby. Now, here we are together. The name feels right."

Oros stepped in closer, looking down at the baby dragon stoically. "You honor Jessie's memory," he said.

Skylet looked up at him, and for a moment, he couldn't look at her. Then he finally turned to see her face, thinking of his mother.

"Let us go home," Séya said. She picked up baby Ulonae and wrapped her up in the edges of her robes, walking toward the water.

35.

Since he had traveled to Mysteya by boat before, Oros led the way back to town. They traveled along the outskirts to avoid the townspeople. It had already been such a long day that the thought of encountering anyone else, and having to explain the baby dragon they carried with them seemed overwhelming.

Soon, they made their way up to the mountain and, ultimately, the cave that was once Jessie's home.

Once inside, Oros looked around in awe of the spacious chamber. Séya prepared a makeshift bed for the baby dragon and gently laid her down near a grassy patch.

"This is where you have been all these years?" Oros asked Skylet.

"Yes," she said, before turning to Séya. "I'm going to find some berries for her to eat."

"That's a good idea," Séya replied.

Skylet walked away, stopping for a second to watch the two of them, the old woman speaking softly to the little hatchling, her voice trembling at certain moments.

It was obvious that Séya was thinking of Jessie, the longest friendship the old woman had. She had lost more than a mentor and a friend. She lost a sister; a soul connection—one who understood with her heart in a way that words could never even hope to do justice.

Skylet could see the old woman wiping the tears away from her face as she doted on the baby dragon. She tried desperately within herself to make sense of the cave she had known all her life and how different it felt in Jessie's absence, the void so deep nothing could ever hope to fill it. Yet in the dragon's place, Ulonae and Oros had appeared. She would need to make sense of that too. She knew she would need to rely on Séya to help her do that. The girl was also certain that the old woman would be leaning on her to make sense of the significant changes as well.

Skylet turned away from Séya to leave the cave, while Oros stood nearby, watching her. "If you allow it," he began. "I would like to join you."

Skylet stopped and turned to face him. "If you like." She turned away and began walking. Séya watched quietly as the two exited the cave.

Skylet walked outside along a path she knew very well, stopping for a moment to take her boots off and continue walking barefoot. Oros followed a few feet behind her until she found a tree with low hanging branches. Large berries hung temptingly; she began picking some.

"This is a beautiful place," said Oros softly.

"It is," Skylet replied. "Arca and I would run out here looking for berries and tormenting each other." She chuckled a little.

There was silence between them for a moment. The calming, hopeful sounds of chirping birds and a gentle breeze called to mind the notion of a future beyond the weight of recent events. It was enough to get Oros thinking about what that future might look like. He hadn't the slightest idea; he wasn't even sure he deserved to see it. The thought of it terrified him in a way that facing even the toughest dragons never did. Yet, he hoped somehow, that he would be gifted with the opportunity to help build that future. If there was any small chance, he felt compelled to take it. "Skylet," began Oros.

"Yes?"

"I understand this is a trying time," he said, struggling with himself. "I want you to know that. . . that you still have a brother," he paused, letting the weight of that sentiment fall where it may. "That is, of course, your decision."

Skylet didn't respond. She continued picking berries.

"I would like to know the woman my sister has grown into."

She reached a branch that was too tall for her and looked up at it for a moment as though it would lower itself closer to where she could touch it. "Could you help me reach that group of berries?" she asked.

Oros stepped in and picked them for her, along with some others that were higher. They walked farther along the path and came to a cliff that overlooked a lower verdant valley behind the mountain.

Skylet took a seat on a rock near the cliff and looked up at Oros, who was standing behind her, holding the freshly picked berries.

"All right," she said, releasing a breath that suggested both exhaustion from everything that had transpired and the relief of being back home.

Skylet turned away from him and looked out over the valley, letting the afternoon sun warm her. Oros took a seat next to her and followed her gaze. The two of them did not speak. Instead, they searched themselves in the silence for a way to become comfortable in each other's presence, not knowing how they would accept the new roles presented to them.

"Oh!" Oros began. "I want you to have something."

Skylet looked at him quizzically.

With his free hand, he removed the talon necklace from around his neck and held it out to Skylet. "Take this," he said. "I no longer need it."

Skylet looked at the talon that hung from the necklace in Oros's hand and then looked up at him, noting his genuine expression. "Are you sure?" she asked.

"I am," he replied.

She reached out to collect the talon. When she closed her hand around it, the cloak she wore reacted, flapping as though a burst of wind blew through it. The cape moved with such force that it knocked Skylet over on her side, causing her to drop the berries she picked. The dragon skin garment began to calm itself until it stopped moving altogether.

"Are you okay?" Oros asked, surprised, quickly getting up to help her.

Skylet didn't respond immediately. She stared at the claw in her hand before unraveling the necklace, getting herself back to her upright sitting position. She put it around her neck as she slowly began picking up the fallen berries. "Yes," she said. "I am."

"Are you sure?" Oros asked, touching her shoulder. "That was a strong push."

"Yes. Jessie. . ." she paused. "Jessie is all right too. I can almost feel her more strongly now." The thought made her emotional. While she let a few tears fall, she didn't fully give herself over to crying. Though she missed the dragon's physical presence, something inside her felt like a puzzle had been completed. She couldn't fully understand or articulate it, but she knew it felt comforting, almost peaceful.

Oros knelt with her and wondered what questions he might ask next to learn more about her. Skylet had questions too, but she knew she would need time before she felt comfortable enough to ask them.

Her mind briefly wandered to baby Ulonae. She wished Jessie could see how beautiful the little dragon was, as she considered the new changes in her family. Skylet understood that Jessie's spirit was indeed present, and she tried to find solace in that. She considered everything the dragon taught her, all the moments they shared, and tried to be grateful for all the gifts she had received. Even Oros himself felt like a strange gift from the dragon, one she wasn't sure how to accept just yet.

She decided to trust Jessie's love. Something told her that everything would work out in a way that could be healing for them both. But for now, she needed to sit and look out over the valley and feel the breeze. When she was ready, she would begin getting to know her family anew.

36.

It was late in the evening. Skylet, Séya, and Ulonae had all gone to sleep in the cavern wall where Jessie used to rest. Neither of them mentioned it, but they wanted to feel close to the dragon. Her scent was still strong there.

Since baby Ulonae wouldn't be coming into contact with another dragon anytime soon, they thought perhaps being around the smell of a dragon would somehow calm her in moments when she seemed restless.

Of course, Séya knew all about uneasy little ones, having handled many babies in her lifetime. The one thing she found universal among baby dragons and children alike was that they all got agitated and threw tantrums from time to time. The only difference between the two was that there was less a chance of getting burned by children.

Meanwhile, Oros lay awake in the grass bed at the center of the floor, listening to the mellow sound of the waterfalls resonating throughout the cave. Unbeknownst to him, he occupied the very spot that Skylet had so many years ago when Séya brought her there in the wicker basket as a baby. That night was to be the start of her new life with a sorceress and what many would consider a fire-breathing beast. Similarly, Oros was beginning his new life with the very same sorceress, a dragon, and now a long-lost sister who was no longer lost.

He allowed himself to ruminate on dragons as he lay looking up at the cave ceiling. Though he had always respected the power and majesty of them, he found it challenging at that moment to reconcile his past. For much of his life, he had seen the creatures as enemies. He had trained for years to hunt and kill them, and now he would be spending a lot of time with the hatchling Ulonae, watching her grow and learn about the world around her. There was something touching about that to him. Yet, the contrasting ideas of who he used to be and who he was now free to become seemed to clash within his mind. It was the very thing keeping him awake.

Soon, his thoughts wandered to Skylet and how a dragon and a sorceress brought her up. He shook his head at how absurd that would sound to someone else. The outside world, Oros thought to himself, might have an easier time digesting an orphan child having been raised by wolves rather than a massive creature that could fly and a magic-wielding woman. After all, what would the world come to if children grew up with such a strange pairing of guardians?

Still, Skylet had seemed well adjusted enough. Having spent her whole life around dragons, loving and caring for them, she didn't grow up to become some wild animal without humanity. As far as he could tell, her spirit was true, and her character was as honorable as his Uncle Servalan's.

The thought of this made his heart feel softer; he didn't fully know what to make of it yet. Soon, he found himself contemplating his mother and how proud he thought she might be of her daughter.

Then there was the matter of the sorceress. Oros thought that growing up with a sorceress did not seem to corrupt Skylet either. As one who throughout his life had been indifferent to magical folk or to the whispers of such people, he never obsessed over how being magical was frowned upon and carried punishments of the most severe kind. The thought just never crossed his mind.

Now, after weathering life-and-death experiences in one intense day with Séya, Oros found himself wondering what his own childhood might have been like had he crossed paths with her sooner.

He was glad that Séya had found Skylet as a baby and took care of her. The thought of it made him smile to himself, which surprised him. It seemed to have been ages since he had genuinely smiled.

A groaning coming from deep within the cavern in the wall caused him to sit up. Skylet was having a bad dream. It pained Oros to hear her sounds of anguish; he wished he could change whatever she dreamt of so that she could rest peacefully.

Just as he started to lie down again, he began to hear bodies stirring. He could tell that Séya was speaking in a soothing tone, but he couldn't make out what was being said.

Something began rustling from inside the cavern, the sound making his body tense. Yelps from Séya and squeals from a now wide-awake hatchling were enough to cause Oros to grab his sword from nearby and spring into action. He quickly made his way up the wall and into the cavern, entering the space to find Séya dancing around holding Ulonae in one arm and trying to avoid being hit by Skylet's flapping and expanding cloak. "Jess," she said soothingly, raising her free hand toward the cape. "What is it?"

Skylet was still asleep on the floor, turning and groaning, and reaching for whatever she saw in her dream.

"What is going on?" Oros asked, his weapon drawn.

Séya calmly put out her dragon-free hand toward Oros to prevent him from moving in.

"She is all right," the old woman said.

"Are you certain?" Oros was uncomfortable.

"*Nnnnnoooooo!*" Skylet suddenly screamed in her sleep, her arms flailing, her feet kicking every which way. "Jessie! Don't go away! *Jessieeeeeee!*" She awoke and sat up, breathing heavily; sweating. "Jessie," she said to herself quietly. Her tone was one of deep sadness.

Séya reached out and touched the garment, which had begun to calm down. Ulonae was now crying and squealing following the commotion. "Come," she said, motioning to Oros to join her.

He leaned his sword against the wall and moved toward Séya.

"Here," she said. "Hold her, please." She handed baby Ulonae to him.

He stood, awkwardly holding the squirming dragon.

"Move your arm this way," Séya stepped in to help him comfortably hold her. "There you are."

Ulonae nestled herself in the pocket of his arm and her wailing began to subside.

Séya gently touched his shoulder before turning her attention to Skylet, who had her head in her hands, crying. "Dear child," Séya began softly, tightly wrapping her arms around the girl.

"Jessie. . ."

"I know, dear."

Skylet looked up at Séya, sniffling. "Jessie is trying to tell me something." The girl was shaking now.

Séya blinked. "What do you suppose it is?"

"Where the others are," said Skylet. "It was all so real, more than anything I've ever dreamt." She sounded frustrated that she couldn't see more before waking up.

"What is the meaning of it?" Oros asked, rocking Ulonae as gently as he could. "Who are 'the others'?"

Séya and Skylet looked up at him.

"The rest of my family," said Skylet. "The other dragons."

ACKNOWLEDGMENTS

It seemed that there were many forces at work, attempting to prevent me from writing this book. It took a lot to get here and, so many people helped along the way.

I extend my sincere thanks to the wonderful and passionate team at Atmosphere Press for taking a chance on this story. Nick, Bryce, Cammie, and Ronaldo, I call you out. Your work on this book, from the fantastic cover design to sound suggestions on the text, and most importantly, your patience throughout a challenging time as I worked to get my pieces together, have been invaluable.

Ms. Viannah, I thank you so much for your eyes and your comments through another pass of this book.

To Linda, thank you for giving me the crazy idea that this book was publishable.

G-Money, I am beyond grateful for the fruitful discussion and excitement from you about this story. So much more to tell you, but for now, you are fantastic, always. Rhubarb and, of course, Janeblessings.

Mirabel, you were the first real human in the outside world to learn this book would be real and no longer just a manuscript. I'm beyond grateful for your kindness, your endless support, creative inspiration, and your genuine friendship throughout this journey. We are coming!

Rozina (Liv), I don't have enough words. Thank you so much for being my partner at the 16th precinct all these years, for supporting my writing, and the very notion of this book on the side. I love you, dear.

To Ms. Angelica, you already know. Thank you for your support, for so many laughs, dealing with my boring voice for hours, and for putting up with those early chapters you claimed were well written. You are the realest.

My Starseed spirit sister Jewels, you are one of my heroes. I feel so fortunate every day that the universe reconnected us. Thank you so much for reading those first chapters and for all the rich and thought-provoking conversation. Most of all, thank you for being you. I told you we weren't done. <3

To Ms. Claire, it overwhelms me how seen I have been by you. Thank you for your beyond beautiful words on the first bits of this story and for sharing your heart, thoughts, and spirit with me. I look forward to exchanging even more letters with you!

Darci, your support, care and encouragement mean the world to me. Thank you so, so much. <3

Dear, dear Kellie. My fellow wordsmith, and wonderful friend, I love and respect your being, as I have these many years I've known you. I cannot properly put into words how pivotal you were in shaping this story. Truly. Without you, the book doesn't reach this stage. Period.

Your pointed comments, eagle-eyed examination of the text, insightful suggestions, and unadulterated excitement for this tale were the right nudge I needed at just the right time. It has been easily one of the greatest and most humbling of honors to work with you. You really took special care with this story, and I'm so grateful. Bless you, dear. And that, is the point. G-Squared Shows 4 Life.

Jerry, I honor your memory here. What a gift it was to know you for the time we had. Your encouragement and support on this book and my writing continue to carry me. You are very much missed.

Mary, thank you for always believing in me and for

planting the idea that I could have a book in a bookstore somewhere. I wish you could see this.

To my CIIS family, who helped further shape my creative self: Carolyn, Randall, and Cindy, I am forever grateful for your support around this book and your support of me. Thank you for being the best.

To my cohort sisters Christie and Pauline: Christie, I cannot thank you enough for your encouragement with the process of the last legs of this book and for always meeting me wherever I am on the line of our shared wavelength. I love you.

Pauline, you continue to hold my heart and hold space in this book in ways that weren't apparent to me in the beginning. Thank you for staying connected with me from the ethereal place. I love you, as well.

My cohort brother Nate, I am overwhelmed by your love and support; you have my love too. I look forward to sharing this and more with you.

Rudith, you know what time it is. Thank you for trying with this book when there was space to. For offering ideas and taking peeks at the text. I love you.

Dad, thank you for your encouragement.

Mom, you read that clunky first draft, and I love you for it. Thank you.

Nik Nak, thank you for reading the early sketch of the story when there was nothing else and for supporting me as I figured it out. <3

Pat, thank you for your support. But if the cops weren't here. . . Love you.

Marty Mar, thank you for letting me talk your ear off about this process. I love you too. "Oh yeah, I used to be a salesman. It's a tough racket."

Dria, I love you. Thank you for cheering me on all the time. Shadalaou.

Big Zion and Na to the Naar, for all the support, laughs and love, thank you so much! I love you!

Asa Ace is the place. You remain one of the most influential people to acknowledge here. I'm blessed to know you and to have been inspired by your energy. This book doesn't exist without you. Thank you so much. I love you.

To any dear reader who has braved these words and made it this far, I thank you so, very much. You have taken the time to read this book and I'm grateful. Seriously. I hope that you found it worthwhile in some way. Be well.

ABOUT ATMOSPHERE PRESS

Atmosphere Press is an independent, full-service publisher for excellent books in all genres and for all audiences. Learn more about what we do at atmospherepress.com.

We encourage you to check out some of Atmosphere's latest releases, which are available at Amazon.com and via order from your local bookstore:

Newer Testaments, a novel by Philip Brunetti
American Genes, a novel by Kirby Nielsen
All Things in Time, a novel by Sue Buyer
The Red Castle, a novel by Noah Verhoeff
Hobson's Mischief, a novel by Caitlin Decatur
The Black-Marketer's Daughter, a novel by Suman Mallick
The Farthing Quest, a novel by Casey Bruce
This Side of Babylon, a novel by James Stoia
Within the Gray, a novel by Jenna Ashlyn
For a Better Life, a novel by Julia Reid Galosy
Where No Man Pursueth, a novel by Micheal E. Jimerson
Here's Waldo, a novel by Nick Olson
Tales of Little Egypt, a historical novel by James Gilbert
The Hidden Life, a novel by Robert Castle
Big Beasts, a novel by Patrick Scott
Nothing to Get Nostalgic About, a novel by Eddie Brophy
Alvarado, a novel by John W. Horton III
Whose Mary Kate, a novel by Jane Leclere Doyle
An Expectation of Plenty, a novel by Thomas Bazar

ABOUT THE AUTHOR

Photograph by Beanie Bear Studios, © 2020

Born and raised in the Bay Area, Steven Armstrong is an award-winning filmmaker, screenwriter, and author. He spent several years in the nonprofit world of maternal health, becoming inspired by countless stories of resilience, while working as an editor and staff writer reviewing films. Steven holds a BA in Creative Arts from San Jose State University and an MFA in Writing and Consciousness from the California Institute of Integral Studies. His work has appeared in the *Samizdat Literary Journal*. When not writing, he might be found making some other art or cooking. *Dragon Daughter* is his first book.

CPSIA information can be obtained
at www.ICGtesting.com
Printed in the USA
FSHW010503160421
80541FS